SAFE PLACE (RAINBOW PLACE #2)

JAY NORTHCOTE

COPYRIGHT

Warning

This book contains material that is intended for a mature, adult audience. It contains graphic language, explicit sexual content, and adult situations.

ONE

Late May

ALEX WAS full of nervous excitement while he hurried to keep up with Hayden, who was striding down the street as if he were on a mission. "I should be back at home revising," Alex protested. "My dad would do his nut if he knew I was out tonight."

"Don't be such a wuss," Hayden said. "Don't you want to go and support Seb? Rainbow Place is the coolest thing to happen in Porthladock, basically ever. It's already late, so we don't have to stay long, but let's just have a quick drink."

"I guess."

Rainbow Place was pretty awesome, and the fact that an LGBT-friendly café/bar was opening right here in Alex's home town was incredible. It gave Alex some much-needed hope for the future. But Alex's dad would go even more mental if he knew where Alex was going tonight. Alex's father was furious that Rainbow Place was still going ahead with its grand opening, despite his vocal opposition to Seb Radcliffe's plans.

Just thinking about his dad's reaction made Alex feel sick, but also sent a thread of steely determination through him. Fuck his father and his stupid, bigoted views. In a few months he'd be escaping anyway, his dream of leaving home to go to university now so close to being a reality. As long as he got the grades he needed he'd be gone by September. Alex needed to keep his head down, stay out of trouble with his dad, and he could survive till then. But that didn't mean he couldn't live a little too. Lucky for him, his dad was too wrapped up in his business and political connections to pay much attention to him. That suited Alex just fine. His parents were out at some Tory party social in Truro that evening and wouldn't be back till midnight. Alex could be home and in bed by then and they'd never be any the wiser.

"Maybe some of the rugby lads will be there again too," Hayden said, casting a knowing sidelong glance at Alex. "Maybe *Cam* will be there."

Cheeks flaming, Alex muttered, "Shut up." But he couldn't help smiling as butterflies exploded in his stomach at the thought.

He'd met Cam earlier in the week when he, Hayden, and a couple of other friends had gone to help out after Rainbow Place had been vandalised. The vandalism had come in the wake of Alex's dad writing a shitty letter to the local paper about the plans for a queer-friendly café. It may not have been directly related, but Alex couldn't help feeling guilty by association. When photos of people rallying around to help repair the damage had gone viral on social media, Alex and his friends had decided to join them.

The scale of the vandalism had shocked Alex. The walls had been spray-painted with horrible, homophobic slurs. He could only imagine how devastated Seb must have been. But the fact that so many people came to help must have softened the blow. It had actually ended up being an amazing night—not least because of Cam.

Cam was part of the local rugby team who had been some of the first to volunteer their time to help clean off the graffiti. Alex and Cam had ended up getting talking while they'd worked side by side on cleaning the kitchen floor, and Alex was smitten.

There was no way Cam would be interested in him though. He'd been a little flirtatious, sure. Enough that Alex had suspected Cam might be gay. Unfortunately, he was way out of Alex's league. Cam was gorgeous: tall, dark, and handsome with a thousand-watt smile and shoulders to die for. He was also clearly a few years older than Alex, and was cool and confident where Alex was awkward and constantly worrying about saying the wrong thing.

"Wow, it looks really busy." Hayden's voice snapped Alex out of the Cam rabbit hole his brain had fallen into.

Standing outside Rainbow Place in the early summer twilight, they paused, and looked through the windows. The place was packed, all the tables were full and people were standing around the bar.

"That's cool, though. Good news for Seb," Alex said.

"There might not be anywhere to sit but we can stand at the bar. If Amber was working I could have got her to try to save us a table or something, but she finished at lunchtime."

Their friend Amber had got a job working as a server there. Alex was envious. He worked Saturdays cleaning the static caravans on one of his dad's holiday parks on changeover day before the next lot of tourists arrived. He'd much rather be working at Rainbow Place.

"I don't think she'd be able to do that unless we were going to eat."

"Yeah, I guess not. Let's go in anyway. I'm thirsty."

Hayden flicked his bleached blond hair out of his eyes as he made his way confidently to the bar. Alex followed a few steps behind. This seemed to be his default position in life in relation to his best friend.

Hayden had realised he was gay a couple of years before had Alex worked out that he was too. Then Hayden came out when he was fifteen, long before Alex even began to think about the logistics of how and when he'd tell people. He'd even had three boyfriends when Alex had only had one—Hayden. But that was only a few months of casual fooling around before they'd decided they were better as friends. They weren't each other's type anyway. Hayden liked his guys older and hairy, and Alex liked his guys taller and more muscular than Hayden who was short and slender.

Following in Hayden's wake, Alex did a quick scan of the room and his heart rate quickened when he spotted Cam at the bar with some of the other rugby players. He looked away, not wanting to be caught staring.

Instead, he focused on Seb, who was behind the bar and smiling warmly at them. "Hey, guys. It's great to see you again. How are you?"

"Good thanks," Hayden replied while Alex gave Seb a grin and a nod. The rugby lads laughed at something. Hoping it wasn't at him, Alex ignored them, but they'd caught Hayden's attention. He nudged Alex in the ribs and said a little too loudly, "Look who's here!"

Feeling like he had to look to shut Hayden up, Alex glanced over at the group again to find Cam's gaze on him.

When he caught Alex's eye, Cam smiled widely, and raised his hand in greeting. Alex tried to wave back casually but was overcome by self-consciousness. He felt his cheeks flame and he tore his gaze away, cursing himself for being socially inept.

He tuned back into Seb and Hayden's conversation. Seb had asked Hayden for ID. The idiot must have tried to order alcohol, which was pretty ambitious given that Hayden looked young for his age.

"Coke then." Hayden sounded disgruntled.

Seb caught Alex's eye and raised his eyebrows in question.

"Same for me please," Alex said.

"Nice try." Seb grinned at Hayden as he poured. "How old are you anyway?"

"Seventeen," Hayden replied. "But not for much longer. I turn eighteen in two weeks, and Alex's eighteenth birthday is in June too."

"Not too long before I can serve you that cider you wanted then." Seb slid the first Coke across the bar and started pouring the second.

Alex had always hated that his birthday was so late in the school year. It was frustrating last year when so many of his peers learnt to drive long before he did, and now it was annoying not being able to buy alcohol legally. At least he only had one more month to wait.

"Final year at school then?"

"Yep." Hayden nodded.

"Shouldn't you be at home revising for your A levels?"

"Don't you start. I get enough of that from my mum. It doesn't matter what grades I get anyway, I already have a guaranteed place on the hairdressing course I want to do next year." Hayden pushed his hair out of his eyes again as he handed some cash to Seb. Once he'd got his change, Hayden turned to Alex. "Where do you want to sit?"

"I dunno." Alex wasn't sure there were any free seats, let alone tables. He didn't fancy squeezing onto a table with strangers. But as he scanned the room he noticed a couple of people standing by one of the two-seater sofas and putting their jackets on. "Oh... those people look like they're leaving, how about there?"

The words were barely out of his mouth before Hayden was hurrying across the room to bag the sofa before anyone else could get to it. Alex followed more slowly, unable to resist a final glance at Cam as he passed. Cam didn't notice. He was busy chatting to one of his friends. Disappointed that they hadn't managed to talk, Alex took a seat beside Hayden. The sofa was comfortable, and there was a coffee table for their drinks.

"This is cool," Hayden said. "I really like this place. Shame about the cider though."

"Yeah." Not that Alex was a big drinker, but a little bit of booze usually helped take the edge off his self-consciousness. Maybe if he'd had a couple of ciders he'd have the nerve to approach Cam and say hi. Or at the very least he'd be able to smile at him without blushing like a tomato.

"Lucky for you, I came prepared." With a covert glance around to make sure nobody was watching, Hayden slipped a small hip flask out of his back pocket and sloshed some clear liquid into both their drinks.

"Awesome. What is it?"

"White rum, nicked from my mum's drinks cabinet."

"Cool. Cheers." Alex took a swig and nearly choked. "Bloody hell that's strong."

"Yep." Hayden grinned. "Oh look, there's Amber."

Hayden waved at her as she passed with a tray of dirty plates. She flashed them a quick grin and disappeared into the melee of people standing around the bar, neatly sidling through them until her spiky dark hair vanished from view. "I thought she'd finished after lunch. She was supposed to be going to the cinema with Sophia tonight."

Amber emerged again a couple of minutes later and made a beeline for their table. "Hey." She stooped to give them both hugs and kisses. "You made it!" she said to Alex.

"Yeah. My parents are out and Hayden persuaded me."

"How come you're still working?" Hayden asked.

"It's been so busy Seb asked me to stay on. So...." She shrugged. "More money. Plus it's pretty awesome in here tonight."

"You should have told Sophia to text us. She could have come out too." Sophia was Amber's girlfriend and they were usually inseparable.

"She had a three-hour essay paper for her English Lit exam today and was knackered. She decided to get an early night."

"That'll be me next week." Alex's stomach lurched with anxiety at the thought of his upcoming exams, and he took a fortifying swig of his rum and Coke. He wished he'd chosen subjects he cared about more. It was hard to motivate himself to revise Maths, Economics, and Business Studies when he'd been pushed into those subjects by his dad. If only he'd had the balls to stand up to his father and study things he actually liked; History maybe, or Sociology. Maths was okay, at least he was good at it, but the other two were boring as fuck.

"I'd better get back to work," Amber said. "Have fun."

Once she'd gone, Hayden got out his phone. "Oh, I got a

message from that guy in St Austell I hooked up with last week."

"The builder?" Alex had heard more details than he needed about how big his dick was and how he'd bent Hayden over the back seat of his SUV.

"Mmm." Hayden was already typing a reply.

Letting his gaze wander around the room, Alex felt the dizzying rush of the alcohol hitting his system. His eyes were drawn to Cam again and his heart did a somersault when he found Cam looking back at him. This time, Alex forced himself not to look away immediately. His lips felt as though they were made of rubber, but he somehow shaped them into a smile, and was rewarded when Cam grinned back before turning to the guy next to him. Alex's disappointment at the loss of connection turned to panicked excitement when Cam excused himself from his group of mates and started to head in Alex's direction.

Oh my God. Be cool. Don't freak out.

Too late. He was already freaking out.

"Hi, Alex. How's it going?" Cam asked, offering a large hand to Alex to shake.

"Not bad thanks. You?" Alex managed, sure that his face was flaming again. Cam made him hot all over.

"Yeah, pretty good. Hayden, is it?" Cam addressed Hayden, who had glanced up from his phone.

"Yes, that's right. Hello. It's lovely to see you again." Hayden held out his hand. After shaking, he said, "Actually you'll have to excuse me. I need a piss. Have my seat if you like." He gave Alex a quick wink that made him blush even harder.

"Cheers." Cam slid into the seat Hayden vacated.

Suddenly the two-seater sofa felt tiny. They weren't quite touching, but Alex was aware of every inch of space between them, and was sure he could feel the warmth of Cam's body. Struck dumb by Hayden's desertion, Alex scrambled around for something to say that wouldn't sound totally idiotic. The booze seemed to have slowed his brain without toning down his awkwardness. "It's busy here tonight isn't it?"

Ugh. State the bleeding obvious, why don't you?

"Yeah. It's brilliant to see so many people here. I reckon Seb must be dead chuffed. This is exactly what he was hoping for—a mixture of queer people and allies just having a cool time."

Alex scanned the room again, studying the customers more carefully. He hadn't been paying much attention before, too distracted by Cam. Now he was looking properly, he noticed the lesbian couple who'd been here on Monday eating dinner together. He also spotted a couple of old guys with grey hair holding hands across the table and smiling at each other. The sight made something twist in his chest, wistfulness tangled with hope.

"It's really lovely to see. Kind of inspiring I guess," Alex blurted. Then felt daft for being so effusive.

But Cam held his gaze and smiled. "Yeah. I know what you mean."

He does?

Cam hadn't volunteered any information about his own sexuality when they'd talked on Monday. Alex had revealed his when he'd had to explain why he didn't want to be in a photo for the paper. He was afraid of what assumptions his father might—correctly—make if he'd known Alex was part of the rescue mission to fix Rainbow Place after it had been targeted. Alex had been desperate to know if Cam was into guys, but it seemed rude to ask.

Apparently, rum disabled Alex's verbal filter, because

before he could think better of it the words were out. "So, are you gay too?" At least it came out sounding vaguely casual.

"I'm bi."

"Oh. Cool." Alex cringed. *Cool?* God, he needed to get a grip.

Grinning, Cam said, "I'm glad you think so." Then he had a sip of his pint while Alex tried to recover from his latest conversational pitfall. He raised his glass too and gulped at his drink, forgetting about the rum until it burnt his throat and made him cough. "You okay there?" Cam patted him on the back, his palm warm and strong. He took Alex's glass away with his free hand as Alex nearly spilled the contents when he coughed again.

"Yeah sorry," Alex managed. "Went down the wrong way."

"What are you drinking?" Cam sniffed the glass. "Rum and Coke?"

Flushing, Alex said quietly, "Yeah. But Seb wouldn't serve us alcohol; he knows we're only seventeen—although I'm going to be eighteen soon," he added. "Hayden brought a hip flask."

"Ah." Cam chuckled. "Been there done that. Speaking of Hayden, he's been a while. Do you think he's okay?"

Alex felt bad for not noticing that Hayden had been gone way longer than it took to have a piss. "I'm sure he's fine." Looking around the room, he spotted Hayden standing at the bar again. It looked as though he'd bought two more Cokes. "Yeah, there he is."

Sure enough, after he'd paid, Hayden headed back to their table. "I thought you might be ready for another."

"It should have been my round," Alex protested.

"You can pay me back another time." With his back to

the bar, Hayden deftly spiked their drinks again. "Here you go. I'm going to go and chat to Amber. Seb said she can finish work now most people are done eating, so she's going to have a drink before heading home. See you in a bit." He sashayed away to rejoin Amber who was sitting on a bar stool.

"How old are you?" Alex asked Cam. It seemed to be his night for asking personal questions, so fuck it.

"Guess." Cam raised his eyebrows in challenge.

"Oh. I hate that game. You always end up offending someone whichever way you get it wrong."

Cam laughed. "No, I don't care either way. I promise. I'm just interested to know."

At least it gave Alex the perfect excuse to study Cam carefully. His skin was clear, so he was definitely over puberty, and although he was clean-shaven there was a shadow that suggested he could grow a full beard if he wanted to. Alex reckoned he was in his twenties, but whether early or mid it was impossible to tell. "Twenty-one," he said finally, hopeful that Cam was closer in age to Alex than he'd initially suspected.

"Nope. Not too far off though. I'm twenty-three."

Six years older; that wasn't an impossible age gap.

Cam held Alex's gaze and there was a frisson of tension between them. Cam gave Alex a smile that was unmistakably flirtatious before asking, "Do you have a boyfriend?"

"No. Do you... or a girlfriend?"

Cam shook his head. "I'm young, free, and single. But I'm quite happy that way."

Alex supposed it was okay being young, free, and single if you got laid regularly as Cam presumably did. It was less fun being young and single if you were a desperate virgin like him. He took a cautious sip of his new drink and forced himself not to wince. It was even stronger than the first one. He was already feeling pretty tipsy, and was finally relaxing around Cam, thank goodness. Deciding a subject change was in order, he asked, "So, what do you do?" It was a boring question, but he was interested to know. He wanted to know everything about Cam.

"I work for a landscape gardening firm."

"Do you enjoy it?"

"Most of the time. I like being outdoors, and it's good having a job that keeps me active. I think I'd go nuts if I was behind a desk all day. But it's a bit boring sometimes. I'd like to get more into the garden design side eventually."

Alex sipped his drink. It was going down more easily now. He wondered how much Cam had drunk tonight. The rugby crowd had been pretty raucous so he guessed they'd been here for a while. Cam's cheeks were flushed, and his eyes were slightly glassy. His lips were moving, and Alex realised he was asking him a question.

"Are you still at school?"

"Yes." Alex hated admitting it. It made him sound so young.

"What do you want to do when you leave?"

"I should be going to university in the autumn hopefully, as long as I get the grades."

"What are you gonna study, and where?"

Wrinkling his nose, Alex said, "Business Studies, and my first choice is Manchester, second choice Northumbria."

"Wow. You'll be a long way from home either way then. You don't sound very excited about it."

"I let my dad talk me into applying for that course. I wish I'd gone for something I was more interested in, but it's too late now. Whatever. At least it's a chance to get away from here and start fresh. I want to come out once I'm at uni. I can't do that while I'm still living at home."

"Your parents won't be supportive?"

Alex's stomach turned over as he imagined his dad's reaction. "No. Do your family know about you?"

"Sort of. I told them, but I'm not sure how seriously they took me. I hook up with guys sometimes, but my parents have only ever seen me with girlfriends so it's easy for them to ignore the fact that I'm bisexual."

Hayden and Amber approached them. "Hey. I think we're gonna head off now," Hayden said. "Do you want to come with us or are you staying a little longer?" He glanced between Alex and Cam with a suggestive grin. "I don't want to break things up, but we're both tired."

Yeah right. Since when had Hayden ever gone home because he was tired? Alex was being set up, and he didn't mind in the slightest.

"I still have my drink to finish, so you guys go on. I'll see you tomorrow."

Hayden grinned. "Okay then. Have fun."

Once they'd left, Cam shifted his position, stretching an arm out on the sofa back behind Alex's shoulders. "I'm glad you stayed," he said quietly, mouth close to Alex's ear. Warm breath sent tingles down Alex's spine.

"Really?"

"Yeah."

Overwhelmed, Alex didn't know what to say next. They sat drinking in a tense silence for a moment until Seb called last orders at the bar, and a few people hurried over to order drinks.

"Do you want another?" Cam asked. His pint was empty now.

"You can't get me alcohol, remember?" Alex didn't

think he needed any more. His glass was mostly ice, the drink all gone, and he was at the perfect stage of drunkenness where he knew exactly what he was doing, and wasn't slurring his speech, but he felt buzzed and happy, and full of confidence.

"Ah yeah, sorry. I forgot you're underage."

"Not for everything I'm not." Alex gave Cam a suggestive grin, simultaneously shocked and thrilled by his brazenness. Hayden would never believe he'd actually managed to flirt. Miracles could happen, apparently.

Cam seemed surprised too. His eyes widened for a moment, but then a slow smile spread over his face. Alex's heart was thumping so hard he felt a little dizzy, or maybe it was Cam's proximity as they held each other's gaze. "You ready to leave then?" Cam asked. The thump of disappointment was brutal, until Cam added, "We could take a detour along the harbour before walking home. I love looking at the boats at night." There was a hint of uncertainty in his expression, as though he thought Alex might decline.

Wild horses couldn't make Alex refuse. "Sounds good." He managed to sound casual—he hoped—but on the inside he was jumping up and down and his heart was doing cartwheels. He checked his watch and saw it was just after eleven. As long as he didn't stay out too much longer he should still make it home before his parents.

"I'll just say bye to the lads." Cam stood, and Alex lingered awkwardly behind; not sure whether he should go with Cam or not. As Cam bade farewell to his rugby mates, Alex spotted Seb behind the bar. He was watching them with a knowing expression on his face. "You okay?" he mouthed to Alex.

Alex nodded, and then went over to him. "Looks like you've had a great day. Congratulations."

Seb beamed. "Yeah. It's been brilliant."

Cam moved in alongside Alex, putting a hand in the small of his back. "You ready to go?"

"Yeah."

"Goodnight, guys," Seb said. "See you soon, I hope."

TWO

Out in the street, the darkness was disorientating at first. After three pints, Cam wasn't pissed, but he definitely felt a little unsteady. Not as unsteady as Alex, though, who stumbled beside him as he missed the step down from the kerb into the street.

"Oops." Alex flailed, until Cam took his arm.

"You all right?"

"Yeah, yeah. Just clumsy."

Cam let his hand slide down to take Alex's in a firm grip. "I'll hold you up." Alex was so fucking cute. He'd captured Cam's attention on the day they'd met, and Cam had been really pleased to see Alex there again tonight. His mates had ragged him for dumping them, but it was all light-hearted. They'd do the same in a heartbeat if there was a pretty girl they wanted to chat up.

At first, Alex hadn't seemed interested tonight. He'd been shy and awkward, and Cam thought maybe he'd misread the signals on Monday. But then suddenly things had changed. Maybe it was the alcohol, but whatever it was,

Cam liked the confident, flirty side of Alex that had emerged later. He was pretty sure they were on the same page, and was hoping this chapter would end with a blowjob if they could find a discreet spot.

They walked along the dark street and took the turning that led to the harbour. Ahead of them, the water reflected the light of the moon. As they walked past The Anchor, the doors of the pub opened and a group of people spilled out, talking among themselves as they walked in Cam and Alex's direction. Alex snatched his hand away and shoved his hands in his pockets. Once they'd passed the group he muttered, "Sorry."

"It's okay. I get it."

When they reached the harbourside they crossed to the paved area that overlooked the water.

"It's so lovely here at night," Alex said dreamily. He slipped his hand into Cam's again, warming Cam with the gesture. "Let's sit for a bit." There was a bench that faced out over the estuary. Cam let Alex lead him there and they sat, still holding hands.

The water shifted like silk in the moonlight and small waves lapped at the harbour wall in a peaceful rhythm. "I love living by the sea," Cam said.

"Me too. It will be weird living inland next year when I go—*if* I go to uni."

"Yeah. A bit different to here." Cam couldn't imagine living in a city. Being brought up in Cornwall he was too used to the sea and sky, beaches, fields, and moorland. He'd been to London a couple of times to visit mates who'd moved there, and it was fascinating. But he wouldn't last a week living there.

"Yes." Alex sighed.

"You want to go though?"

Alex shrugged. Cam felt the lift of his skinny shoulder next to his. "Yeah. Mostly I do. I want to get away from my parents. And I want space to be myself... to feel *safe* being myself."

"Are your parents that bad?"

Cam found it hard to imagine. His parents weren't marching alongside him in any Pride parades—not that Cam had been to one yet—but they hadn't been dicks about it when he'd told them he was bi. His mum had just said, "Good for you, dear, and that's nice that you told us." While his dad had shrugged and said, "Whatever. Just don't get anyone pregnant till you're ready for that."

"They're pretty awful, honestly." Alex shuffled a little closer, whether for comfort or warmth Cam wasn't sure, but he took the hint and released Alex's hand so he could put his arm around him. Alex snuggled closer still, and they looked out at the dark water and the reflection of the harbour lights for a while. A yacht was motoring in to moor for the night, the distant hum of its engine audible over the sound of the waves. "This is so nice," Alex said.

"What is?" Cam asked.

"Being here with you... like this."

Cam studied Alex's profile in the dim light from the street lamps. His nose was straight and his lips full.

"What are you looking at?" Alex turned and their faces were inches apart.

"Just admiring the view," Cam said, and then snorted. "Oh my God, that was the cheesiest line ever. I'm so sorry."

"Shh. Don't ruin it." Alex grinned. "I would say I'd heard worse, but I'd be lying."

"Gee. Thanks."

"No! Only because nobody's ever used a line on me before."

"Okay, well I feel a little better now." Poised on the edge of making a move, Cam hesitated. Alex was young—legal, but still a kid really; and the more time they spent together, the more he suspected that Alex was very inexperienced. Cam didn't want to be the arsehole who pushed him into anything he wasn't ready for.

While those thoughts were going through his head, Alex leant forward and kissed him in a clumsy crush of lips.

Stunned, Cam froze for a fatal second and Alex pulled away, his face stricken. "Sorry, sorry." He slid away from the shelter of Cam's arm. "My mistake. I thought you wanted…. Sorry."

"No!" Cam stopped him retreating further by grabbing his hand. "No, I did want. I do…. You took me by surprise, that's all."

Alex still looked uncertain, so Cam proved the point by cupping his jaw and leaning in slowly to press his mouth to Alex's. Cam loved kissing; it was honestly one of his favourite things to do—especially with guys. He loved the softness of their lips compared to the scratch of stubble. He enjoyed the intimacy of slow, sweet kisses, like the ones he was giving Alex now; but he also liked harder, rougher kisses, the deep and desperate type when you were fucking someone and wanted to fuse your body with theirs in every way possible.

Moving closer, Cam slid his hand into Alex's hair, and smiled as one of Alex's hands came up to touch his face, stroking Cam's stubble with his fingertips. Alex was passive at first, letting Cam lead the kiss. Gradually, he became more confident, copying Cam, and returning the small brushes of lips. Arousal unfurled in Cam's belly, like a flower opening its petals. He kissed Alex more insistently and was rewarded when Alex gave a quiet moan as their tongues touched for the first time.

Cam lost track of time as they snogged. It was a long time since he'd kissed someone like this without taking things further. It reminded him of being a teenager, where he'd make out with someone for hours, but not actually get his hand in their pants. He wanted more, but not here. They might be alone for now, but there could be other people walking home and they needed to be cautious.

Sure enough, the sound of footsteps and voices made Cam start and pull away.

"What's the matter?" Alex asked breathlessly, lips wet.

"People." Cam jerked his head towards the road behind them as another group of people made their way home after a night out.

"Oh shit. I didn't notice."

Grinning, Cam said, "I'll take that as a compliment."

"You should." Alex's smile was sheepish. "I think someone could set fire to this bench and I wouldn't notice." Then he sighed. "I should probably go home soon. I'm not supposed to be out during my exams so I want to get home before my parents do."

"What time are they due back?"

"Around midnight."

Cam pulled out his phone to check the time. "Um..., Alex. It's quarter to midnight now. How long does it take to walk back to yours?"

"Fuck." Alex leapt up. "About ten minutes. I'm gonna have to run. I'm sorry."

"Do you want company?" Cam wasn't ready to let him go yet.

"Yeah, okay."

Alex wasn't kidding when he said he was going to run. They went back through the centre at a swift jog and Alex didn't slow his pace at all when they started going up one of the steep hills that led to the outskirts of town.

"Bloody hell, you're fit." Cam was surprised. Alex didn't look like the sporty type.

"I do cross country at school," Alex said. "It got me out of team sports so it was the lesser of two evils."

Huffing out a laugh, Cam didn't have enough breath to keep the conversation going. It was a relief when the road finally levelled off. Bypassing the housing estates, Alex turned into one of the lanes that were lined with bigger, older houses. There were no street lamps along here, but a few of the houses had porch lights on. Alex stopped in the shadow cast by a large rhododendron that blocked the light from the house behind it. "This is me." He gestured to the house, which was huge and expensive-looking with a beautifully kept front garden. A brand new Range Rover was parked in the driveway. Alex's parents must be wealthy.

"Wow. Nice place."

Alex shrugged. "I suppose."

He looked uncomfortable so Cam changed the subject. "Can I get your number? I'd like to see you again."

"Yeah?" Alex beamed. "Cool, and yes, of course."

Cam got out his phone, unlocked it, opened his contacts, and then handed it to Alex. "Put it in here; I'll message you later."

Still smiling, Alex typed, and then gave the phone back.

"Thanks," Cam said. "You got time for another kiss? We can make it quick this time."

"Yeah." Alex looked back down the way they'd walked. "I'll hear the car when they turn into the street, so I can beat them inside." He faced Cam. Some of Alex's earlier confidence had evaporated and he licked his lips nervously.

"Come here." Cam opened his arms and Alex stepped into his embrace so eagerly that Cam stumbled back, stopped by a waist-high stone wall that bordered the garden. "Steady."

"Sorry," Alex said, and then they were kissing each other again.

With their time together limited there was an urgency to it. Cam's arousal built sharply, nothing like the gentle swell of before and he groaned as Alex fitted himself between Cam's thighs where they were spread slightly. The stone wall bit into Cam's arse, but he didn't care because he could feel Alex's erection hard against his own. Knowing this couldn't go any further tonight was sweet torture, but hopefully another time....

The sound of an engine had Alex jerking away. "That's probably them. I have to go." He pressed one more kiss to Cam's lips, and then he was running, feet pounding as he rounded the corner into the driveway. "Text me!" he called back.

"Will do." Cam started to walk away so he wouldn't look as if he was casing the joint.

The slam of Alex's front door came just as the car—a Porsche—swept past him, slowing, and indicating to turn in. Neither of the people in the car paid Cam any attention, so once it had turned into the drive he stopped, unable to resist the urge to be nosy. He crept back and peered through the edge of the rhododendron just in time to see a glamorous blonde woman climb out of the passenger seat. High heels clicked on the paving as she made her way to the door.

A well-built man got out of the driver's side and Cam froze as he saw his profile in the porch light.

No fucking way. It can't be.

It was.

Cam's stomach churned. *Holy shit.*

Alex's dad was none other than Martin Elliot: local millionaire, business owner, ex-UKIP candidate, now Tory supporter, and all-round bigoted arsehole. Not only that, but he was also the person who had written a vile letter to the press to stir up opposition to Rainbow Place.

Sharp sympathy cut through Cam. No fucking wonder Alex didn't want to come out till he left home when the poor kid had that wanker for a father. Shaking his head, Cam hurried away into the night.

WHEN CAM GOT BACK to his place, his friend and housemate, Wicksy—Simon Wicks to people who weren't his friends—was snoring in front of the TV with an empty plate covered in crumbs on his lap, and a half-full bottle of beer on the coffee table.

Sitting on the sofa beside him, Cam said, "Oi, you lazy fucker. You going to finish that beer?"

"Huh?" Wicksy jolted awake. "Oh. It's you."

"Who the hell did you think it was going to be?" Cam snagged the bottle of beer and took a swig. He needed to settle his nerves after the revelation of Alex's family connections.

"What happened with Alex?" Wicksy asked, muting the television. "Did you get off with him?"

"Sort of."

"What does sort of mean?"

"Just a snog."

"Ah. So you came home to me all horny instead? Shame you're shit out of luck there." Wicksy grinned. "Mind you, it would be good if I swung that way. We'd make excellent fuck buddies."

"Your arse is way too hairy for me to want to fuck it," Cam shot back. He was used to Wicksy's brand of humour and he could give as good as he got.

"How come you didn't get more than a snog then? I could have sworn the kid was into you."

"Don't call him a kid; it makes me feel like a creeper. He's only six years younger than me and he's over the age of consent."

"Yeah, yeah. Whatever. I'm not judging. So what happened then?"

"He had to get home."

"You going to see him again?"

"I dunno." Cam frowned and had another mouthful of beer.

"You not keen anymore?"

"It's not that. I definitely fancy him, and he's a really nice guy too.... But his dad is Martin Elliot."

Wicksy's eyes flew wide and his jaw dropped in a way that would have been almost comical if the reason for his surprise wasn't still twisting Cam's guts with unease. "Oh fuck!"

"Yeah. Exactly." Cam sighed heavily. "So, much as I like Alex, I'm not sure I want to risk getting in the middle of that. He's not out, and has no intention of coming out till he leaves home. Normally, that would be fine by me. I can do discreet. But what if we slipped up? What if his dad found out?"

"Yeah, sure, mate. That could be ugly. I don't blame you for wanting to steer clear."

"Plus I think Alex has enough on his plate with exams coming up, and a homophobic tosser for a dad. I'm not sure hooking up with me would make his life any less complicated. I think he could maybe use me as a friend more than a boyfriend."

"Who said anything about a boyfriend?" Wicksy raised his eyebrows. "That sounds a bit serious for you."

"Yeah, yeah." Cam's cheeks heated. He didn't know how the word "boyfriend" had popped out. "You know what I mean though."

"Well that's very noble of you, mate." For once, Wicksy didn't sound as if he was taking the piss. "And you're probably right. Seems like he's already dealing with a lot."

"Trouble is, I think he likes me." Cam's phone was burning a hole in his pocket. He knew he should text Alex to check he'd got in okay without any hassle from his parents, but he wasn't sure what else to say. "I got his number, and told him I wanted to see him again. But now...."

"Now you don't."

"Well, I do wanna see him again. But I think it's best if it's only as a mate, and I'm pretty sure he was hoping for more." Like Cam had been hoping for more till he realised who Alex's dad was.

"You'll have to let him down gently. It's not like you haven't had plenty of practice at that."

"Yeah." It was true. Cam had lots of experience in giving the "let's just be friends" speech—usually with girls, but sometimes with guys too. It wasn't that he was an arsehole; he was just averse to commitment so tended to cut and run before things had a chance to get serious.

He drained what was left in the bottle and put it back on the coffee table, and then stood. "Okay, I'm going to head up to bed. See you in the morning."

"Night." Wicksy put the sound back on the telly and

settled down to watch it. Cam would give it five minutes before he was asleep again.

Once he was in bed, Cam typed a text to Alex.

Cam here. Hope you got in okay. Sleep well. He read it back, trying to judge if it was friendly enough without leading Alex on. Deciding it would do, he hit send.

Knackered and ready to sleep, he turned the sound off on his phone and was about to set it aside when a reply flashed up. *I had fun tonight. Thanks.*

Me too, Cam replied, unable to resist the temptation to reply immediately even though maybe he shouldn't.

When can I see you again?

Normally Cam liked it when people were up front about their interest. If it was mutual it was good to move things along, and if it wasn't—well, better to be honest about that too. But with Alex things weren't clear cut. It was so tempting to ignore his sensible head and follow his instincts. Cam was drawn to Alex, and after kissing him tonight, he was pretty sure they'd have good chemistry if they took things further. But no.

You free tomorrow? Let's meet for a chat and take it from there. Cam didn't want to let Alex down by text, he felt he owed him an explanation, but he didn't want to give Alex false hope either.

Okay :) Goodnight

Night. Cam muted his phone and set it screen down beside his bed. Lamp off, he settled under his covers and closed his eyes. He remembered Alex's tentative kisses, and the passion that had built between them as they'd given in to it. Then, *damn*, that last kiss before Alex had heard his parents' car. Cam let his hand slide down to squeeze his cock through his boxers as he imagined what they might have done if they'd had more time.

No.

Jerking off thinking about Alex wasn't going to help his resolve tomorrow. He pushed the thoughts away and left his dick alone. Horny and unsettled, he tossed and turned for a while before finally managing to sleep.

THREE

Alex woke on Sunday morning full of nervous anticipation about seeing Cam later. His stomach fluttered and dick hardened as he pictured Cam, and remembered how it had felt to kiss him. He'd wanked last night as soon as he'd got home, but was ready for round two of Cam-fuelled fantasy.

As he stroked his cock, Alex closed his eyes and let vague images drift through his mind of things he wanted to try: sucking Cam's dick, Cam sucking his, jerking each other off while they kissed....

Alex came with a muffled grunt, spilling over his fist, and splashing onto his T-shirt.

Breathless, he opened his eyes and smiled at the ceiling, happiness and excitement rising and making his heart pound. Maybe he'd get to do some of the things he'd imagined soon—maybe even today if there was somewhere private they could go. He wondered what Cam's living situation was, because there was no way Alex could invite him here unless his parents were out.

After a quick shower, Alex went downstairs to get some

breakfast. The smell of coffee permeated the air. His parents were already up and sitting at the kitchen table. His mum was reading on her Kindle and his dad was on his laptop.

"Morning, Alex," his mum said.

"Morning." Alex went straight to the bread and put two slices in the toaster.

His dad didn't look up from his laptop. He was scrolling with a scowl on his face. "I don't understand why so many people are supporting this ridiculous venture. It looks as though it was packed out for the opening night."

Hand on the fridge door, Alex froze.

"What's that, darling?" his mum asked.

"This bloody gay café. I don't get the appeal. There are photos all over Facebook and it looks like half the damn town was there yesterday."

Alex's stomach lurched. He hadn't seen anyone taking photos while he was there, but what if he'd been caught on camera? Forcing himself to act normally he got out some orange juice. His hand trembled as he poured it into a glass.

"I'm sure it will be a flash in the pan success. The novelty will soon wear off," Alex's mum said.

"I hope so. Or maybe it will be vandalised again." His dad snorted. "At least there are clearly *some* other people in the town who have issues with it."

Gritting his teeth, Alex put the juice away. His dad had made no secret of his delight when Rainbow Place had been targeted at the start of the week. He'd been positively gleeful about it. That was part of the reason Alex had been so determined to go to help.

Relieved that there was a lull in his parents' conversation, Alex spread his toast with butter and jam, and then picked up his plate and his glass of orange juice and carried them towards the kitchen door.

"Don't you want to eat at the table?" his mum asked, eyebrows raised. She'd finally lifted the total ban on Alex eating in his room when he'd turned sixteen, but she still didn't approve of it.

"No. I've got loads of revision to do, and I want to get started as soon as possible." It was true. Alex had three exams coming up this week, the first on Tuesday, and he definitely needed to study.

"Well make sure you bring your plate down later."

"Of course." With that, Alex escaped to the sanctuary of his bedroom.

It was sad how much time he spent avoiding his parents. Not that most of his mates spent huge amounts of quality time with their mums and dads either, not at their age, but Alex disliked being around his more than the average teenager. Dinner time was the worst. His mum insisted on them eating dinner "as a family," which meant them grilling him about his schoolwork, or him having to listen to their right-wing, xenophobic, LGBT-phobic views on anything happening in the news.

Sitting at his desk, Alex got out his Economics file and started half-heartedly reading through some of his notes. It was hard to concentrate when he was on tenterhooks waiting to see if Cam would text him. He opened his messages and re-read their exchange from last night. He was worried he'd sounded too keen, but Cam was the one who'd asked for his number.

Maybe he should text Cam? He didn't have to sit around and wait, but he'd sent the last message before bed, so perhaps it would look pushy if he made first contact today.

Ugh. Alex knew he was overthinking, but it was impossible not to.

At half-eleven he was saved from his distracted attempt at revising when his phone chimed. Nearly knocking it off his desk in his haste to grab it, Alex's heart leapt when he saw it was from Cam.

Hi, how are you today?

Good thanks :) You want to meet up later? Alex typed, and then he had second thoughts and deleted the last part before sending.

Cam's next reply read: *Wanna meet for a coffee or something today?* Alex did a little fist pump, glad that Cam had been the one to ask.

Yeah, that would be cool. What time, and where?

How about the café at Skinner's Cove. 2pm? Cam suggested.

Perfect, Alex replied.

OK, see you then.

Alex sent back a thumbs up and his phone remained silent after that. He set it aside with a smile on his face and fluttery excitement in his stomach.

SKINNER'S COVE was a sandy beach flanked by rocky headland on either side. Just north of Porthladock and an easy walk from Alex's house, it was a popular spot with tourists and locals alike, and the café was open all day.

Too keyed-up to hang around at home any longer, Alex got there half an hour early and found a sheltered spot by the sea wall near the café where he could sit in the sunshine. It was one of Alex's favourite places, although he and Cam wouldn't have any privacy here on the sand. Alex had been hoping for more snogging at least; maybe they could find somewhere quieter.

While he was waiting, Alex let his mind wander as he watched the people on the beach. It was breezy and cool, despite the sunshine, so lots of the adults were huddled behind windbreaks while their offspring played in the sand or ventured into the water to emerge shivering if they weren't wearing wetsuits. Older kids were scrambling over the rocks at either end of the beach, looking for crabs in the rock pools that were uncovered as the tide went down.

Despite growing up here, Alex had rarely come to the beach with his family as a child. His dad was always too busy working or playing golf with his business or political associates, and Alex's mum hated the beach. She preferred taking Alex to the sterile outdoor swimming pool at the local health club where she could sit on a sun lounger while Alex played in the water under the watchful eye of a life-guard. On the few occasions she'd begrudgingly taken him to the beach for an hour or so, she'd spent all her time sitting on a blanket reading, and complaining whenever he'd acci-dentally kicked sand on it.

Once Alex was twelve years old, he'd been allowed to go to the beach on his own, or with friends, and he'd made up for lost time. The beach was his sanctuary away from home and he loved it in all weathers and seasons. Perhaps he loved it best of all in the winter when he sometimes had it all to himself. When the sea was rough he could sit and watch the waves for hours, the rhythmic roll, crest, and crash as they broke on the beach soothing and hypnotic.

When it was almost two o'clock, Alex relinquished his place by the wall and approached the café, nervous tension ramping up. Resisting the urge to pace, Alex sat on the wall on the edge of the slipway instead. From this vantage point he could see the road sloping up towards the town.

He recognised Cam as soon as he rounded the corner even though he was still quite a distance away. Watching him approach, Alex couldn't believe they'd actually kissed last night. Tall, muscular, and perfectly proportioned, Cam looked as if he'd stepped out of the pages of a catalogue. A pale grey T-shirt showed off his tanned arms, and navy shorts revealed muscular legs. Cam was so hot, it seemed incomprehensible that he could be interested in someone as nondescript as Alex. It wasn't that Alex was ugly or anything, he was just... normal-looking: average height, average build, mid-brown hair that had just enough wave that it was a nightmare to style, and annoyingly pale skin that burnt way too easily.

Not expecting Cam to notice him, Alex was surprised when Cam raised his hand and made a beeline for where Alex was sitting. "Hi." He gave a smile that made Alex's stomach swoop.

Standing quickly, Alex brushed sand off his denim shorts. "Hi."

Alex wondered if he should offer his hand, or go in for some kind of hug, or what, but he left it too late and Cam didn't make a move to touch him, instead he asked, "Do you want to get a drink or something?"

Alex nodded. "Yeah. Sure." Ordering would give them a focus to get them past the first few awkward minutes.

There were a couple of families in front of them, which gave them time to read the menu on the chalkboard behind the counter. "What do you want?" Cam asked. "I'm buying."

"You sure?"

"Yeah."

Alex wasn't in the mood for coffee, and he fancied an ice cream more than anything, but didn't want to look like a kid in front of Cam. "What are you going to have?"

"It's too hot for coffee, maybe a smoothie."

"Oh, a smoothie sounds nice." Not quite as good as a chocolate ice cream cone, but definitely better than bitter coffee.

"What flavour?"

"Um... mango and raspberry, please."

They waited in silence after that. Alex wanted to try to initiate a conversation but felt self-conscious with other people close by. Cam's quietness was a little disconcerting too. On their other meetings, he'd been the one who'd got Alex talking and put him at ease.

Once they had their drinks they sat at one of the picnic tables in front of the café. There was an umbrella for shade and Cam took his sunglasses off, so Alex followed suit. Their gazes locked for a moment and Alex's cheeks flushed hot. Arousal zinged through him as he remembered how Cam's hard body had felt pressed up against his last night. Looking away quickly, Alex took a sip, and then stirred his smoothie with the straw. The silence between them was far from comfortable and Alex was desperate to break it because it didn't seem as if Cam was going to.

"Thanks for this." Alex lifted his cup and glanced at Cam again.

"You're welcome."

"Maybe I can buy you one another time," Alex said hopefully. He'd read somewhere that confidence was supposed to be sexy. Cam was here after all. If he hadn't wanted to see Alex again he wouldn't have asked for his number, or messaged him, or suggested they meet today, would he?

"Yeah, maybe." Cam smiled, but there was something about it that was strained.

Alex's heart plummeted into his gut, taking away his appetite for the smoothie. He hated this sense of foreboding. All his optimism of earlier had melted away because Alex wasn't being paranoid. Cam was definitely being weird, and not his usual friendly self.

"Look, if this was a mistake, just say," Alex blurted out, keeping his voice low because the last thing he wanted was anyone listening in if this was about to end badly. "If you regret what happened last night, I'd rather you told me and got it over with."

Cam eyes widened. "No, it's not that." Hope flared in Alex's chest before Cam doused it again with his next words, "But we need to talk properly. Sorry, this probably wasn't the best place to meet for a conversation, was it?"

"No." Alex's voice was scratchy, as though his throat was lined with sandpaper.

"How about we walk up the coast path for a bit, there'll be way less people up there."

"Okay." Wanting to get this over with, Alex stood immediately. He drained his drink, the icy mixture making the roof of his mouth ache. Crushing the cup, he tossed it in the bin as he passed it, heading for the steps that led up to the path.

The cliff path snaked up steeply away from the beach into a patch of woodland. Too narrow for them to walk side by side, Alex led the way with Cam on his heels, walking quickly. As soon as they were in the cool, green cover of the trees, Alex said, "So. What did you want to say to me?" He knew he sounded defensive but couldn't help it. Pretty positive the outcome wasn't going to be good for him, he wanted Cam to spit it out already.

"I want to be able to see you for this conversation," Cam said, a little breathless. "Can we stop somewhere and sit for a while?"

"If you want." Alex pushed on even faster. He knew the perfect spot. After a few minutes he took a barely visible overgrown path that branched off to the left. They followed that for about fifty metres until they passed a warning sign that read: *Steep drops. Danger of death.* Just after that, the path emerged onto the concrete top of a WW2 bunker built into the cliff. Alex turned to Cam. "Will this do?"

"Yeah. What a cool place. I can't believe I didn't know about this."

Alex took a seat on the sun-soaked concrete, his back against the rock of the cliff face. Cam sat beside him, close, but not touching. Waiting for him to speak, Alex ached with longing as he stared out at the postcard-perfect view of the headland opposite, separated from this side of the river mouth by the deep blue water. He'd never understood the term lovesick before, but his desire for Cam was like a physical illness.

"So... last night wasn't a mistake," Cam said, his voice calm and measured. "I don't regret it. I like you a lot, Alex, and I enjoyed what we did." Alex waited as he paused, heart thumping hard. "But I think it's best if we keep things as just friends."

Letting his breath out in a rush, cold disappointment was balanced by a hot rush of frustration. Alex glanced sideways at Cam, then down between his knees. He picked up a piece of rock and scratched ineffectually at the concrete. "But if you like me, and you enjoyed fooling around with me, then why? You're the one who said you wanted to see me again, and I know you didn't mean just as friends then, so what's changed? Or were you wearing beer goggles last night and now you've sobered up you realised you don't actually fancy me after all?" Alex didn't care if he sounded whiny and desperate. He was pissed off and wanted Cam to be honest with him.

"Because I saw your parents, Alex. I know who your dad is."

Oh. Alex's stomach rolled. He couldn't meet Cam's eyes, shame filling him because of his dad and what he stood for. Even though he suspected he was fighting a losing battle, Alex made a last-ditch attempt. "So? Yeah, my dad's an arsehole. What does it matter? You don't have to meet him."

"I'm sorry, Alex." Cam's voice was gentle. "I just think you have enough to deal with if you're hiding your sexuality from a man like your father. Plus, you should be focusing on your exams so you can get away from him in September, yeah? I don't want to make your life more complicated than it already is."

His kindness was a pin that burst the balloon of Alex's bluster, leaving him deflated, eyes full of humiliating tears that he tried to blink away. "But nobody would need to know. Please, Cam." He finally turned to meet Cam's gaze. His eyes were blue like the water far below them, his expression soft and full of regret.

"I'm sorry, Alex. But I've made up my mind."

The pity on his face was unbearable. Gritting his teeth, Alex flung the piece of rock in his hand out over the water and watched as it spun in the air, arcing before the inevitable fall. To his shame, he felt a tear escape, tracking hotly down his cheek before he dashed it away.

"I'm sorry," Cam said again. "And for the record. I meant it when I said I want to be friends; that wasn't me letting you down gently. I think you're a cool person. If you aren't totally pissed off with me for messing you around, I'd like to carry on hanging out with you."

The seconds ticked past while Alex debated. Did he want Cam in his life if he couldn't have him in all the ways he wanted? Emotion was a hot fist in his chest, but as time stretched out, it slowly unclenched, making it easier for Alex to breathe again. He turned back to Cam. Hope was written in every line of his face.

"Yeah. I want to be friends," Alex said gruffly. Although Alex wasn't short of friends, it was always good to have more. It might be cool having an older queer friend too—like a kind of mentor. Alex's crush would pass eventually, and then it would be easier.

Cam smiled. "Good." His stomach growled then, making them both laugh, and breaking the tension. "Sorry. I was too nervous about this conversation to eat lunch earlier. Wanna head back to the beach café and get some chips?"

"Sure." Alex scrambled up and offered a hand to Cam. Even if they were only friends, he couldn't resist taking the chance to touch him. He pulled him up and they stared at each other for a moment, hands still clasped together. Alex craved more contact.

"Hug?" Cam asked, as though he could read Alex's mind. "Friends can hug."

Alex nodded. "Yeah." Cam opened his arms and Alex stepped into his embrace. Warm and comforting, Cam smelt of citrus shampoo and fresh sweat. Hugging him back, Alex breathed him in, absorbing Cam's strength until he was ready to let go. "Okay, let's go get those chips."

Cam led the way back down the path to the beach and Alex admired his broad shoulders and tried not to focus on his butt, because now they were only going to be friends that felt a little creepy. Disappointment was still lodged in his stomach like a rock, but Alex would find a way to deal with it. He'd had enough unrequited crushes on boys at school to know he could handle it. Being friends with Cam was definitely better than nothing, especially if hugs were involved.

FOUR

June

CAM WAS PLAYING on the Xbox with the sound turned low while Alex read through his revision notes. He'd brought his books over to Cam's to study tonight because his parents were out. Cam liked having Alex in his living room, even when they were busy doing their own thing. He enjoyed his company and quiet presence.

True to his word, Cam had focused on being the best friend to Alex he could since the night they'd kissed. Still feeling guilty for backing out of more, Cam made sure to cultivate their relationship.

Alex had been stressed with exams and revision, so Cam encouraged him to relax when they were together. If the weather was good they got outdoors, hanging out on the beach, walking, and sometimes running together. Cam wanted to keep up his fitness ready for the start of rugby season in the autumn, and Alex was a keen runner—as Cam had found the night they'd run up the hill from Rainbow Place.

When it rained, Alex came over to Cam's place and they played on the Xbox instead, or watched TV. They'd been good at keeping things non-sexual, with no deliberate contact other than hugs of greeting or farewell. Yet Cam looked forward to those hugs. He loved how Alex's lean frame felt pressed up against him, and the way the hugs always lasted just a little too long to be strictly platonic. When they played video games or watched TV, they sat close, knees or elbows brushing. Cam always resisted the temptation to put an arm around Alex. He knew that would be crossing the line he'd drawn between them and it wouldn't be fair to muddy the waters. From the way he caught Alex looking at him occasionally, he suspected Alex's feelings for him hadn't changed.

Cam's hadn't either.

If anything they'd got stronger. The more he got to know Alex, the more he liked him. He was smart, funny, and sweet, and although he was a few years younger than Cam he was mature for his age. Cam's attraction to Alex grew along with his affection. He'd thought he was cute the first time they'd met, but now he appreciated things he hadn't noticed on first glance: the sprinkle of freckles the sun had brought out on Alex's nose, the way he used his hands for emphasis when he talked, the fullness of his lips, and the way he chewed on his lower one when he was stressed, or concentrating—like now.

They had Cam's place to themselves tonight, because Wicksy had gone out for a drink with some of their rugby mates. They'd asked Cam too, but he'd cried off when Alex had texted to see whether he could come over.

Busy with studying, occasionally Alex would sigh, or

huff in frustration, and his bottom lip was pink from him worrying it with his teeth. After a particularly heavy sigh, Cam paused the game, and set his controller down. "Can I help? Maybe test you or something?"

"Yeah. If you don't mind that would be great. It's really fucking boring though, so apologies in advance."

He wasn't wrong. There were pages of notes about operational objectives, operational performance, and productivity. It was all Greek to Cam, who'd left school at sixteen. He'd got decent GCSEs, but hadn't studied any of this jargon-filled nonsense. By the time he'd run through some of it with Alex he still wasn't any the wiser as to what it all meant.

Alex knew quite a lot of it, but there were definitely some bits he was less sure on. "Do you want to go over the human resource stuff again?" Cam asked.

"No." Alex took the papers out of Cam's hands and stood to put them back in his file and pack his bag. "I can't face doing any more now. I'll sleep on it tonight and have a last look in the morning." He stretched and then winced, rolling his shoulder, and rubbing his neck.

"Are you sore?"

"Bit stiff. Too much hunching over a desk, but not for much longer." Alex gave a small grin.

"Well, not till you start uni anyway." Cam ignored the lurch in his stomach at the thought of Alex leaving Porthladock.

"Yeah." A shadow flitted over Alex's face. "*If* I start uni." He hadn't been very positive after some of his exams. The Maths had gone well, but he'd been worried about his first Economics paper. He had one more Economics and one Business Studies paper to go.

"Come here." Cam spread his legs where he sat on the sofa and pointed to the floor between his feet. "Sit."

"Why?"

"I'm gonna give you a massage. Get rid of some of that tension in your muscles."

Alex hesitated for a moment, chewing on his lip again, before seeming to come to a decision. He sat where Cam had indicated.

"Take off your top," Cam said.

After another brief pause, Alex stripped off his T-shirt, revealing the flawless skin of his back. Despite their regular trips to the beach his skin was still milky-pale. He normally wore a rash vest, claiming there was no point in trying to tan because it wouldn't happen. Cam had to admit he had a point, even his arms, which were often exposed to the sun— albeit with high-factor lotion on them—were still only slightly darker than the rest of him. His hair had been cut last week and was shaved short at the back. The skin of his neck was smooth and inviting and Cam had a sudden intense desire to kiss it.

Shit. What was I thinking?

Cam hadn't had ulterior motives when he'd suggested a massage; he'd only wanted to make Alex feel better. But now he was poised ready to touch all that tempting skin, he realised it was going to test his self-control to the limit. His heart was pounding and his breathing was audible in the silence. Hurriedly, Cam picked up the remote, switched to TV mode, and channel-hopped until he got to a wildlife programme about butterflies. That would do. Anything to distract him.

Finally, he laid his palms on Alex's shoulders. They were wide, but not as broad as Cam's. His muscles were lean rather than bulky, and Cam felt delicate knots of bone as he stroked slowly up towards Alex's neck. His skin was warm, and Cam's hands caught a little, so he used less pressure. It would have been easier to do this with oil or lotion but he didn't want to break the tension that buzzed around them, dangerous, and addictive.

Using his thumbs, Cam focused on one side first, gently working the tight muscles in Alex's shoulder and neck.

"God, that feels good." Alex let his head drop forward. As Cam dug a little deeper, Alex moaned, and the sound went straight to Cam's dick. It stiffened in his boxers, stretching out along his thigh where it was trapped.

Shifting his attention to Alex's other shoulder, Cam gave it the same treatment, and was rewarded by the same response from Alex. Did he realise he was making sex noises? He couldn't bring himself to tease Alex about it; Cam was enjoying his sounds too much.

Way too much.

The sound of the front door being unlocked didn't register with Cam. It wasn't till Wicksy burst in saying, "Alright, lads, how's it going?" that Cam realised, too late, they'd been busted. Wicksy's eyebrows nearly hit his hairline. "Ooh this looks cosy. Hope I'm not interrupting anything." He winked at Cam.

Alex jerked away from Cam's hands, the back of his neck flushing pink as he reached for his T-shirt.

"You're not." Cam glared at Wicksy. "I'm giving Alex a massage because he had a sore neck."

"Aw, that's cute. How bromantic." Wicksy knew damn well there was nothing going on between Cam and Alex. He also knew Cam still regretted that in some ways.

As Wicksy threw himself down into the armchair and turned his attention to the TV, Alex stood to put his T-shirt back on, and Cam couldn't help noticing the bulge in his jeans.

Realising his boner was visible too, Cam tried to adjust it subtly. But as Alex's head emerged from his T-shirt, his gaze flickered down to Cam's hand before Cam had time to snatch it away from his crotch. Alex sat beside Cam on the sofa again, and crossed his legs in a way clearly designed to hide his predicament. Thank fuck Wicksy was watching the TV rather than them. "What the hell are you guys watching? Can I see if there's anything better on?" He grabbed the remote and started flicking through the channels without waiting for a reply, settling on some chat show where an actress was being interviewed. "Oh, she's hot. This'll do."

"I should probably head home anyway," Alex said. "It's late and I have a morning exam."

Checking his watch, Cam realised it was half-eleven. The evening had flown by. "I'll see you out." His cock was under control now, and he wanted a moment alone with Alex to say goodbye.

On the doorstep, Cam gave Alex his usual hug, but kept it briefer than usual. He didn't want to get hard again and make things more awkward. "Sorry about Wicksy."

"It's fine. Thanks for the massage." Alex's lips curved in a smile that made Cam imagine them wrapped around his dick. Damn, he needed to stop letting his mind go to those places.

"Did it help?"

"I think so." Alex rolled his shoulders. "It was very distracting, that's for sure." He held Cam's gaze boldly and grinned. Cam hadn't seen this side of Alex since the night they'd kissed. The temptation to respond in kind was overwhelming. But then he reminded himself that Alex had an exam tomorrow. Now was definitely not the time to mess with the parameters of their relationship, not when Alex's future was on the line. "Good." He took a step back, putting some much-needed space between them. "That's good."

Alex's smile faded, but he looked more resigned than disappointed. "Okay, well I'd better get going."

"Good luck tomorrow," Cam said.

"Thanks. Oh... that reminds me. Do you want to come out for drinks on Friday night? Amber has her last exam then, and that's all of my mates finished, so we're going out to celebrate." He paused, flushing as he added, "It's actually my birthday tomorrow too, so that gives us an extra reason to party on Friday. I can't go out tomorrow because I have my last exam the day after. Of course, you might not want to hang out with a bunch of teenagers, but I thought I'd ask. You can bring Wicksy if you like."

"Your birthday? You kept that quiet," Cam said. "I'd love to help you celebrate, and I'm sure Wicksy will tag along. He's always up for a night out. Where are you going?"

"We're starting at Amber's place at eight o'clock. Her parents are cool. They're going out anyway, and said we can have a few drinks there so we don't need to spend so much once we're out. I'll text you her address."

"Okay. See you then."

CAM TURNED up on Amber's doorstep a little after eight on Friday with Wicksy in tow. Music was playing inside, the deep pulse of the bass vibrating through the closed door as he rang the bell.

"They probably can't hear the door," Wicksy said when there was no response. "See if it's open."

Cam tried the handle, and sure enough it was unlocked. He led the way in, following the music to the kitchen, where he found Amber, Sophia, and Hayden sitting around the kitchen table, which was littered with bottles of alcohol and mixers along with a bucket of ice.

"Oh hey, Cam!" Amber greeted him with a huge smile. She had a murky-looking red drink in her hand with a cocktail umbrella and two straws sticking out of it. She put her drink down and got up to give Cam a hug. "How are you? It's great to see you. Alex will be so pleased you came. Hi, Wicksy." She moved on to hug him next.

"Hi, guys." Hayden raised his glass to them. Sophia smiled and waggled her fingers in greeting.

"Where is Alex?" Cam asked.

"He's on his way over, he just texted," Amber replied.

"Oh, cool." Cam caught Hayden's eye and noticed his amused expression.

"Help yourselves to drinks, guys." Amber gestured to the kitchen table. "We're on cocktails as you can see. Google a recipe or make up your own."

"We brought some beer," Cam said. "You should have told us you were doing cocktails, and then we could have brought something more interesting."

"Let me stick those in the fridge." Amber took them from Cam and whisked them away.

Wicksy was already perusing the selection of bottles, so Cam thought he might as well join the cocktail crew. He clearly had a little catching up to do.

By the time Alex arrived, Cam was halfway down his first drink. He'd made a Long Island Iced Tea and was already feeling the effects. Amber had brought in a couple of extra chairs, and Alex collapsed in the empty one next to Cam, flushed, and a little breathless. "Hi, everyone. Sorry

I'm late. Dinner with my parents took ages and then I had to wash the dishes before I was allowed out."

"Happy belated birthday," Cam said with a grin. He handed Alex a gift bag. "It's nothing very exciting, but...."

"Oh cool, thank you." Alex pulled out a pair of running socks and a bottle of rum. "I'm going to leave this in the bag so we don't end up drinking it all tonight."

"Speaking of which, would you like me to make you a drink?" Cam asked. Alex looked like he was ready for one.

"Yes please." Alex smiled gratefully.

"What do you want?"

"Anything. Whatever you're having."

Cam picked up an empty glass and started fixing Alex's drink.

"So, how did your last exam go, Amber?" Alex asked.

"I think it was okay," she replied. "It's so hard to tell though."

"Yeah," Alex agreed. "Waiting for the results is going to suck."

"How long till you get them?" Cam handed Alex his drink. "It's in August, yes?"

"Cheers," Alex took the glass and had a sip. "Bloody hell that's strong. And yeah, the middle of August. Nearly two months away."

"Can we stop talking about exams?" Hayden said. "The whole point of tonight is that they're *over*, and we get to party." He stood and started swaying in time to the music. "Amber, put some dance music on. This is too slow."

Amber picked up her phone and scrolled, "Oh, I just found the playlist you made for my last party. That'll do."

"Woo hoo!" Sophia grinned and jumped up as the opening line of "Born This Way" echoed out of the speaker that was on the kitchen counter.

Amber joined her and Hayden, and Cam and the others watched as they started dancing, arms in the air, and huge smiles on their faces. "Alex, come and dance." Sophia held out a hand to him and Alex let himself be drawn into the circle.

"You coming too?" Alex looked over his shoulder at Cam and Wicksy.

Cam joined him immediately, the group parting to let him in. Wicksy hung back. "I'm not drunk enough for this. I'm way too straight to dance unless I'm totally bladdered."

"Aw poor little straight boy," Hayden crooned. "Come here, baby. I'll show you how to move."

Rolling his eyes, Wicksy went over to Hayden who put his hands on Wicksy's hips and tried to guide him. "Like this. You need to kind of roll them. Imagine you're fucking me."

"No offence, mate. But I don't think that's going to help me get my groove on. You're pretty, but you're not my type. I'm into girls—pussy, not penises for me please."

Cam chuckled at Wicksy's crass joke before realising too late that nobody else was laughing. He glanced at Alex, trying to work out what had just happened and followed Alex's gaze to Sophia, whose smile had vanished. Nothing like the happy, carefree girl of a few moments before, her face was set and her eyes glittered, body still and tense instead of moving with the music.

"Not all girls have pussies," she said. Then she stalked over to the table and picked up her drink. Amber followed her and put an arm around her, murmuring something Cam couldn't catch. Suddenly things slotted into place and Cam understood her reaction and that of her friends.

"What the fuck just happened?" Wicksy was frowning,

totally bewildered. Nobody was dancing now, and the atmosphere was pained. "Cam? What's going on?"

Cam shook his head. It wasn't his place to explain anything to Wicksy. "Just drop it, mate."

"I'm a trans girl," Sophia said, turning to face Wicksy. She held her head high, challenge in her gaze. "Transgender. A girl with a dick."

Wicksy's jaw dropped, and then he flushed an ugly shade of red. "Oh fuck."

"Yeah," Hayden said.

"I'm really sorry. I didn't mean to be an arse. I had no idea." Wicksy's cheeks were still pink and he looked as though he wanted the ground to open up and swallow him.

"I know." Sophia shrugged. "You just didn't think; most people don't. At least you apologised." She smiled then, and Cam was blown away by how pretty she was. "Forget about it. Let's dance some more." Putting her drink, down she took Amber's hand and led her back into the space they were using as a dance floor. Amber put her hands on Sophia's waist, and Sophia looped her arms loosely around Amber's neck. They grinned at each other as they started to move in a sexy rhythm, bodies close, foreheads touching.

Hayden went back to teaching Wicksy to move his hips, leaving Cam and Alex dancing awkwardly together—but not together. Cam would have liked to move closer, to pull Alex into his arms and see how their bodies fit together, but he knew it was dangerous. With the attraction between them still simmering beneath the surface, they couldn't play at dirty dancing. It would be too real.

RAINBOW PLACE WAS RAMMED when they got down there at about nine-thirty. Smokers had spilled out onto the street and were standing around chatting, drinks in hand. Inside, all the tables were full so their group made their way to the bar where there was standing room and a couple of bar stools that the girls managed to snag.

Seb was behind the bar with his boyfriend, Jason, who'd taken to helping him out on busy nights. Jason spotted Cam and the others as they arrived and greeted them with a friendly smile and a wave. He nudged Seb who turned and smiled too. "Hi, guys. We'll be with you in a minute."

They ordered separately rather than buying a round. Amber got drinks for Sophia and herself.

Wicksy offered to buy one for Hayden. "I owe you for the dance lessons."

Hayden laughed. "I'm not sure I helped much. I think you're a lost cause, mate. But thanks, I'll have a Southern Comfort and lemonade."

"Ouch." Wicksy grinned. "Well, at least you tried."

"Can I get you a drink?" Cam asked Alex. "We are celebrating your birthday after all."

"Yeah, okay. I'll have a pint of lager please."

"Which one?"

"Whichever is weakest. I'm feeling pretty wasted from the cocktails, but as this is my first legal drink in a bar it would seem a shame to have something non-alcoholic."

Seb made a show of examining Alex's driving licence, holding it up to the light and studying Alex till he blushed and ducked his head away laughing.

"Okay. It seems legit." Seb grinned and started to pull Alex's pint. "Happy birthday."

They stood near the bar for a while, until some people finished eating and Amber managed to get their table. There were only four chairs but Wicksy had found Drew, their rugby team captain, and Luca—the head chef at

Rainbow Place who'd just knocked off for the night—at the bar and was busy chatting to them.

"I'll see if I can find another free chair," Cam said.

There was a stool free a few tables away and he carried it back, putting it down next to where Alex was sitting and squeezed in beside him. Alex glanced sideways as Cam sat and gave him a shy smile.

"You okay?" Cam asked. The other three were chatting noisily among themselves.

"Yeah. Bit pissed, but fine."

"I think you're supposed to be a bit pissed when you're celebrating your eighteenth birthday. I don't remember much about mine, but I do know I was sick in a flower bed, so you're doing better than me."

Alex chuckled. "Yeah. I'm definitely planning on keeping my dinner on the inside."

"Very wise."

"How does it feel to be legally an adult?"

Shrugging, Alex said, "No different at all. It's rather anticlimactic. But I guess it's cool to finally be able to have beer in a bar." He raised his glass. "Cheers."

Cam clinked his pint lightly against Alex's. "Cheers." They both took a sip. "So what are you going to do with yourself now exams are over? You got any exciting holiday plans between now and when you get your results?"

"No," Alex said glumly. "I'm going to be hanging out here and doing a bit of work for my dad."

"Yeah? What sort of thing?"

"Helping out at one of his holiday parks. I already clean out some of the static caravans on Saturdays, but I'm going to start doing the toilet and shower blocks during the week too. I'm going to be doing about ten extra hours a week." Alex didn't look thrilled at the prospect.

"It'll be good to earn some money though, right? Save some up for when you go to uni." There was that lurch again at the thought of Alex going away. Even Manchester, his first choice, was a good five or six hours drive away. Cam guessed Alex wouldn't be back to visit very often. But once Alex was out of the closet, maybe they could start some-thing—even if it was a very long distance thing?

"I suppose. Assuming I actually go to uni this year." Alex frowned. "I'm not sure I'm going to get the grades I need."

A tiny, shameful part of Cam couldn't help hoping he was right. He overcompensated by saying cheerily. "I'm sure you'll be fine."

"I wish I shared your optimism. Anyway, can we talk about something else now?"

With perfect timing, Hayden turned to them and demanded. "Kill, fuck, or marry. The Hemsworth brothers."

"Can I fuck all of them?" Alex asked, while Cam said, "I don't know which are which, but I'm pretty sure none of them are my type."

"Hmm, yeah. I guess they're not." Hayden glanced at Alex, and then back to Cam with a sly grin. "And no, Alex. You can't fuck all of them. That's greedy."

"Kill Luke, fuck Chris, marry Liam then," Alex said.

"Okay, okay. I've got one for you, Cam." Sophia fixed him with an intense gaze as if she was about to ask some-thing incredibly important. "Donald Trump, Vladimir Putin, and Theresa May."

"Oh Jesus." Cam rolled his eyes. "Really?"

FIVE

Alex was happily buzzed with what felt like exactly the right amount of alcohol in his bloodstream by the end of the evening. He congratulated himself on drinking enough to feel awesome while also managing not to get totally plastered. Sure, he'd probably have a bit of a headache in the morning, but nothing terminal.

They were still playing Kill Fuck Marry when Seb had to ask them to drink up and leave. They were the last customers to go—Wicksy had gone home already. Seb was trying to usher them out of the door into the night while Amber badgered him, "But, Seb, come on. Just tell us quickly. "Tinky Winky, Homer Simpson, and SpongeBob SquarePants?"

"I'm going to have to sleep on it," Seb said firmly. "I'll let you know tomorrow when you come in for your shift at two, Amber. Now please drink lots of water before you go to bed. I can't afford to be short staffed on a Saturday night. If you try and call in sick, I won't believe you."

The others laughed while Amber pouted.

"Slave driver," she grumbled, but she gave Seb a hug

and a kiss on the cheek before he closed the door behind them.

They walked up the steep hill together, but parted ways at the top. Hayden, Amber, and Sophia heading in one direction, and Alex in the other.

Alex hugged each of his friends, extra affectionate from the booze. "You guys are the best," he mumbled as he clung to Hayden.

"Love you too, man." Hayden ruffled Alex's hair and gave him a kiss on the cheek.

Cam was keeping his distance, but Alex wasn't having that. Cam needed a hug too. He might not be such an old friend as the rest of them but he was special.

"Come here. I want to hug you too."

Cam hesitated. "Do you want me to walk you home?"

Alex's heart beat a little faster at the question. He'd love a chance to be alone in the dark with Cam. "I don't mind." He shrugged, trying not to sound too keen. "It's out of your way, and there's no need. But if you want?"

"Yes, walk him back," Hayden said. "Otherwise he might end up in a ditch after all that Long Island Iced Tea earlier."

"I'm fine," Alex protested. "You and Amber are way more pissed than me."

"Yeah, yeah. But you have a handsome man offering to walk you home. Say yes, even if he only wants to be friends."

"Shut up, Hayden." Amber whacked him on the shoulder.

"Ouch! Well it's not a secret, is it? They clearly still fancy each other so the whole thing is ridiculous and they should just stop pissing around and fuck."

Alex's cheeks flamed and he was glad nobody would

notice in the near dark of the street. He didn't dare catch Cam's eye. Even though they'd been trying hard to make the friendship work, their attraction to each other already felt like an elephant in the room whenever they were together. Now Hayden had shone a spotlight on it, it would be impossible to ignore.

"Okay, let's go." Amber grabbed Hayden's arm and started dragging him in the direction of home. "You coming, Cam?"

"You should go with them," Alex said. "I'll be fine."

Cam hung back. "No. I'll walk with you. I know Porthladock isn't exactly the inner city. But after what happened to Rainbow Place it doesn't hurt to be careful."

"Yay!" Hayden said loudly, clapping his hands. "Go for it."

"Shut *up*, Hayden." That was Amber again. "Night, guys."

"Night."

Darkness swallowed up Alex's friends, and as the sound of their footsteps faded, Alex and Cam stood in awkward silence.

"Sorry about Hayden," Alex said.

"It's fine. I don't mind."

"Shall we?" Alex gestured in the direction of his home.

Cam fell into step beside him as he started walking. It wasn't far to Alex's from where they'd parted ways with the others, and he tried desperately to think of something to talk about now he had Cam all to himself at last. Hayden's teasing had made him self-conscious and his mind was blank.

By the time they'd passed the newer housing estates and turned into Alex's road they were still walking in silence.

Fuck it. It wasn't like it wasn't obvious even without Hayden's unhelpful matchmaking.

Deciding he had nothing to lose at this point, Alex said, "Hayden's right though, isn't he?" Cam stopped in his tracks and Alex moved to face him. The only light was from the moon, but it was bright tonight. They stared at each other, and Alex tried to read Cam's expression with no success. Frustrated, he blurted, "He is though. Please tell me it's not just me. You're still attracted to me, right?" Cheeks burning, heart pounding, he waited.

"Yeah," Cam admitted, voice low. "But nothing's changed."

Alex gave a huff of frustration. Turning on his heel, he strode away leaving Cam hurrying after him.

"Alex. Wait!"

Alex stopped abruptly in the shadow of a large chestnut tree with broad leaves and wide spreading branches that blocked what little light there was from the moon. Cam stood right behind him. Alex could hear the rasp of his breathing, so close it sent a tingle down his spine.

Reckless and needy, Alex wheeled around and reached for Cam, pulling him into a hug. He pressed his face into the warm skin of Cam's neck, breathing him in hungrily. "I just want you so much," he muttered. "I can't keep pretending I don't."

Cam groaned. "This is such a bad idea." But he tightened his arms around Alex.

"I don't care." Alex dragged his lips over Cam's stubbled jaw, seeking his mouth.

They found each other in the darkness, soft lips on soft lips, achingly sweet at first, but soon turning into something hot and desperate. Aware they were standing in the middle of the pavement, Alex tugged Cam away from the road towards the low wall that surrounded the property on the corner.

"What are you doing?" Cam asked.

"Shh." Alex kissed him again. "Getting us somewhere a little more secluded." He took Cam's hand. "Come on." Alex climbed over the low wall into the front garden of the corner house.

"What if they have security lights or an alarm or something?" Cam hesitated, his hand still in Alex's with the wall separating them. "We might get caught."

"They don't. Or they do…. But the lights only come on if someone is much closer to the house than this. We'll be fine. I just wanted to get off the path." He tugged Cam's hand, and finally Cam followed him over the wall.

"Here." Alex stopped by the trunk of the chestnut tree where they were screened from the road by some shrubs. Leaning back against it, he pulled Cam back into his arms and kissed him again. He felt Cam's hesitancy at first, but soon he was kissing Alex back just as hungrily as before. Arousal rose in Alex like the swell of the tide. He reached down to adjust his cock where it was trapped, hard and aching in his clothes. The back of his hand brushed over Cam's erection and Cam moaned, pressing into the touch.

Alex grabbed Cam's hips and pulled him closer. Cam spread his legs a little, evening out the height disparity so they could grind against each other. "God that feels good," he murmured, hot breath a delicious tickle on Alex's neck.

"Yeah," Alex gasped, grinding harder. "Wish we could do more. Want you so badly." He brought his hands to Cam's fly and tugged on the button. "Can I?" He wasn't even sure what he was asking for. He just knew he needed more, was craving to see how Cam felt in his hand… or maybe in his mouth.

Cam lifted his head from Alex's neck and glanced around them. "Yeah," he whispered hoarsely. "Go on."

Unfastening Cam's jeans with clumsy fingers, Alex's balls ached. He reached into Cam's underwear and curled his fingers around hot, smooth flesh. Thick and hard in his hand, Cam's dick felt amazing.

As Alex started to stroke, Cam reached down and rubbed his palm over Alex's cock. "You want me to do this for you too?"

"Fuck, yes," Alex said.

Nothing could have prepared Alex for the sensation of Cam's large hand wrapping around his cock and squeezing. He gasped, and when Cam started to jerk him off in earnest he couldn't hold back an embarrassing moan. It was Cam's lips brushing his earlobe that was Alex's undoing. Before he could stop himself, or even warn Cam, Alex was coming, shooting between them, and making a mortifying sticky mess.

"Shit, shit, shit. I'm sorry," he muttered. "I wasn't expecting to come so fast. Fuck, it's gone everywhere."

Cam chuckled. "Yeah, it really has." He released Alex's cock and wiped his hand on his jeans.

Alex tried to help him clean up, but without tissues it was impossible to do anything useful. "Oh God, it's all over your shirt. I'm so sorry."

"It's fine, Alex. Don't worry about it."

"And you didn't even come. Do you want me to...?" He tentatively reached for Cam's dick again to find it had softened to a semi with all the distraction.

"No, I think the moment has passed." Cam gently batted Alex's hand away and rearranged his clothing.

Cheeks burning with embarrassment, Alex tucked his

cock away too. Utterly deflated in more ways than one, he muttered, "I'm sorry," again.

"Alex." Cam caught hold of his chin and tilted his face up so he could press a chaste kiss to his lips. "Stop apologising. It happens. And it's kind of flattering to be honest."

"Yeah?" Alex managed a small smile.

"Yeah."

"So, can we try again another time? Maybe at your place where we have some privacy?" Alex asked hopefully.

There was a long pause that made his heart sink.

Not again.

Cam sighed. "I'm sorry, Alex. I told you this was a bad idea. Nothing's changed. I like you, but—"

"You don't need to explain," Alex said. "I remember the reasons. I shouldn't have pushed tonight. Can we forget this ever happened? Especially the part where I came all over you after about five seconds of dick touching?" He valiantly tried to make it into a joke, even though his heart felt like an eggshell that had been crushed underfoot.

"If that's what you want."

"Yes. I don't want to make things weird between us again. Tonight never happened." If only it was that easy. Alex knew he'd replay it over and over again in vivid detail —both the good parts and the awful parts.

"Okay."

"Right." Alex squared his shoulders. "I'd better get home." He led the way back over the wall to the street then turned to face Cam. "I'll see you soon, I guess."

"Yeah. Call me, and come over soon to hang out—you know you're welcome any time." Cam moved forward and pulled Alex into a hug.

Alex hugged him back, squeezing tight, and trying to ignore the welling feelings of hurt and disappointment that were threatening to overwhelm him. He was the one to pull away, wanting to go to bed and lick his wounds in privacy. "Okay, night then."

"Night, Alex."

Alex turned and fled.

Once he was ready for bed he lay in the darkness for a long time. Wide awake despite the lateness of the hour and the alcohol in his system, he cursed his impulsiveness in making a move on Cam tonight. Their tentative friendship had blossomed into something precious despite the shaky start. It had been stupid to risk that. He had to hope they could go back to hanging out and enjoying each other's company despite their little slip-up tonight. Alex's main regret was that he hadn't made Cam come too.

Oh God. The memory of him shooting his load all over Cam made his whole body burn with humiliation. Alex buried his face in his pillow, wishing he could bury that mental image as easily.

Yeah, it was definitely something best forgotten.

SIX

Mid-August

ALEX WOKE EARLY with a sick feeling in his stomach before he remembered why. The realisation that it was A level results day hit him like a bucket of icy water.

Fuck.

If he was honest with himself, he knew he hadn't put in as much effort as he should've. It was hard studying when you weren't interested in the subjects you'd chosen. Plus he'd spent way too much time daydreaming about Cam during exam season. He had to hope he'd done enough, because although he wasn't excited about the prospect of doing a degree in Business Studies, Alex was more than ready to leave home. Perhaps it would be possible to change to a different course once he got to uni?

The idea that he might not get into uni at all was something he hadn't allowed himself to consider.

While Alex was forcing down some cereal to try to

settle the queasy anxiety in his stomach, his mother sat opposite him reading the *Daily Mail*.

"This whole transgender thing is madness," she said, shaking her head. "Why are so many teenagers suddenly deciding they need hormones? Teenagers are hormonal enough already, that's probably why they're so confused."

"I think most trans people are very sure, actually, Mum," Alex said, trying to keep his voice polite rather than confrontational. If his dad had been there he wouldn't have bothered to challenge her. "And it's not exactly easy for them to get access to hormones anyway."

"I still think it's wrong, giving hormones to teenagers. We should be paying for therapy instead. Look at your friend Daniel. Just because he liked playing with dolls when he was little doesn't mean he's a girl. Maybe he's gay? Not that that would be much better."

Alex stiffened, heart pounding. He clenched his fists under the table and said as calmly as he could, "She's called Sophia, and she *is* a girl. She's also a lesbian—so yes. She's gay." Sophia wouldn't mind Alex saying that; her relationship with Amber wasn't a secret. Thankfully both of their parents were supportive—unlike Alex's.

Her eyebrows shot up, and then she frowned as though trying to slot the pieces of what he'd just said together. Alex expected smoke to come out of her ears any minute as her small-minded neural circuits blew, overloaded by queerness. "Well I still think it's wrong. What if he changes his mind when it's too late?"

"I have to go." Alex stood, picking up his half-eaten bowl of cereal. What little appetite he'd had now completely gone. He emptied the milk into the sink and then scraped the mushy cereal into the food waste bin.

"What time are you going to collect your results?" his mum asked.

"School's open from nine so I'll go up then." He'd arranged to meet Hayden, Amber, and Sophia at the gate so they could go in together for moral support.

"Good luck," she called after him as he walked out of the kitchen.

"Thanks."

He needed it. The breakfast table conversation had made him all the more desperate to get out from under this oppressive roof. Surely he would have at least managed the grades for his second choice. He needed two As and a B for Manchester, but only three Bs for Northumbria.

ALEX MADE it up to school by ten to nine. It was a breezy day. The blue sky was already clouding over and he felt a few spots of rain on his face as he waited. His phone chimed with a text and he pulled it out to find a message from Cam.

Good luck today, bud. Fingers crossed for you.

Smiling, Alex replied: *Thanks.*

His heart twisted at the thought of being so far away from Cam next year if he got the grades. They'd made their friendship work despite the difficult start and the subsequent bump in the road when Alex had made his drunken pass at Cam. After that night, when Alex had embarrassed himself so thoroughly, he'd tried to force himself to stop hoping for more than friendship. He couldn't help the fact that he still fancied Cam, but he enjoyed his company so much he could ignore the occasional flash of longing.

They saw each other a few times a week. Sometimes alone and sometimes with friends. They still went running together, and Alex would often go and hang out at Cam's place in the evening to get away from his parents. Now his exams were over and he was eighteen, there was nothing to stop him going out as much as he liked.

Rainbow Place was their favourite place to go for a drink or a coffee. Knowing he was in an environment where he was safe to be himself felt good to Alex, even if he and Cam were only there as friends. When there were queer couples there, eating a meal together, or chatting over a drink, Alex couldn't help watching them surreptitiously. Seeing two women or two men holding hands, or sharing an affectionate kiss in public gave him hope. Even if he could never have that with Cam, he'd find it with someone else eventually. He was straining against his closet walls, ready to break free as soon as he felt safe.

"Hey!" Amber's voice dragged Alex out of his reverie. She and Sophia were approaching, hand in hand. They'd only recently taken to being openly affectionate in public and there was still an awkward self-consciousness about them sometimes.

"Hi. Where's Hayden?"

"Running late," Sophia said. "He texted. He's on his way. I promised we'd wait for him."

"Ugh. Okay." Alex wanted to get it over with now.

Alex was on tenterhooks by the time Hayden finally arrived, out of breath, and pink in the face. He glared up at the sky, which was totally grey now, the drizzle turning into proper rain. "Bloody rain. Straightening my hair was a total waste of time." He ran his hands through it.

"Seriously, you kept us waiting while you straightened your hair?" Alex rolled his eyes.

"Good hair is important."

"Come on," Amber said. "We're all here now. Let's go."

They joined a tense line of students waiting to collect the all-important envelopes from the school office, and it felt like an age before they got near the front of the queue. "We're gonna go and open them together, yes?" Amber said.

The others nodded.

"Yeah." Alex felt sick again.

When it was finally their turn they stepped forward, the seconds feeling like minutes as the school secretary sorted through the envelopes to hand them theirs one at a time. Once they had them, they hurried to the nearest empty classroom and shut the door behind them.

"Ready?" Hayden said. They all nodded. "Okay. Go!"

Mouth dry, Alex tore into his envelope with shaking hands. So nervous, it took him a moment to make sense of the black ink that spelt out his future. He read, then re-read it, heart sinking as he took in the meaning, dimly registering a happy squeal from Amber and an, "oh thank fuck," from Sophia.

Mathematics: A

Economics: B

Business Studies: D

"Shit," he whispered, collapsing into a chair from wobbly legs. He crumpled up the piece of paper in his fist. "*Fuck!*"

"Alex?" Hayden crouched in front of him, his hands on Alex's knees. "Alex, dude. What did you get?"

Bitter disappointment a lump in his throat, Alex shook his head, and handed the balled-up piece of paper to Hayden who carefully flattened it out. He read it, and then wordlessly passed it to Amber who was standing behind him, Sophia next to her.

"Shit. What was it you needed?" Amber asked.

Alex swallowed hard, but his voice still came out as a

dull croak. "AAB or BBB."

"But point-wise you're only one grade off. If you call them, might you be able to work something out?"

"I got a D in Business Studies. That's the subject I was supposed to be studying." Alex knew it would be a waste of time. There was no way they'd give him a place on that course based on these results. Hot tears threatened but he blinked them back. "How did the rest of you do? Did you get what you needed?" He raised his gaze to look at his friends.

"Yeah," Amber said quietly.

Sophia nodded.

"It didn't really matter what I got anyway," Hayden said with a shrug.

"Well done." Alex forced a smile. "We should go and celebrate your successes, and you can commiserate with me." He knew he needed to work out what the hell he was going to do now, but that could wait till later when he had to face his parents and tell them he hadn't got what he needed to go to uni this year.

"Where do you want to go?" Hayden asked.

"Rainbow Place," Alex said immediately. Being there always made him feel better.

"I KNOW IT'S SELFISH, but I'm glad you're not going to be living hundreds of miles away," Amber said as Alex dug into a slice of rainbow cake.

It was hard to be miserable when you were eating rainbow cake and surrounded by friends, and Alex felt his spirits lift despite his worries about what he was going to do now his plans for the future had been blown out of the water.

"Yeah. I suppose." Alex had often regretted his decision to apply to universities that were so far from Cornwall. He'd done it impulsively one night after a particularly shitty week at home, not thinking about the implications for his friendships.

Hayden was going on to study hairdressing at the college in St Austell and would still be living at home next year. Amber would be fairly close in Plymouth and Sophia was going to Exeter, which was a little further afield, but they'd all still be in the West Country and within easy travelling distance for a weekend. Keeping up contact with his friends would help to soften the blow of being stuck at home while Alex tried to work out what the hell to do with his life.

His phone chimed with a text, and his stomach lurched as he saw it was from his mum.

What did you get? Your dad wants to know too. Text us both please.

He was about to put his phone away, not ready to open that can of worms yet, but then another message arrived.

This one was from Cam and sent a tiny sliver of happiness through Alex despite his anxiety at the thought of facing his parents later.

Alex was glad he wouldn't have to leave Cam. Their friendship was different to that with his other mates. Although they'd kept things platonic, there was an edge to it that made it more precious than Alex's other friendships. He lived for Cam's hugs, and his heart still skipped a beat whenever they met up and he saw Cam's smile. There was a sweetness to their relationship that felt almost romantic. Despite his best intentions, Alex couldn't help holding onto a tiny shred of hope that perhaps eventually Cam might want more.

Is no news good news? Cam's text read.

Afraid not, Alex replied.

Oh, he got back immediately. Then: *Sorry... what does that mean exactly?*

I didn't even get into my second choice.

Fuck. So what are you gonna do?

I have no idea :(

Although Alex knew some of his exams hadn't gone as well as he'd hoped, he hadn't seriously entertained the thought of not getting what he needed. His results were like an earthquake, changing the landscape of the future he'd been imagining for the last year or so.

Want to meet up when I finish work to talk about it? I'll do my best to cheer you up.

Alex smiled, despite everything. *Yeah. I'd love to. Not sure what time, depends on my parents. I'll have to go home and face the music sometime.*

Cool, come as soon as you can get away.

Will do. See you later.

Alex looked up to see his friends watching him as he put his phone away. "What?" he asked.

"That was Cam, I presume?" Amber raised her eyebrows.

"Yeah."

"You're still so smitten." Hayden shook his head, his face serious. He wasn't even taking the piss for once. "And I reckon he is too. I see the way he looks at you when we're out together. Why the hell aren't you boyfriends yet?"

"You know why," Alex said shortly. He'd told his friends everything—except the part where he'd shot his load all over Cam like the desperate virgin he was—and while they understood Cam's reasoning they also sympathised with Alex's frustration.

"Is it good for you to be such close friends?" Sophia asked. "It must be hard."

Hayden snorted, and then covered it with a cough as the others glared at him. "Sorry. I couldn't help myself. Hard is always funny."

"Yeah it is difficult in some ways," Alex admitted, "But the idea of not being friends with him is worse. I like having him in my life."

"Maybe you should start dating other people. It might distract you from Cam and make you realise there are other hot guys out there." Hayden got out his phone and opened a hook-up app. "Look, it's like a buffet of man meat. And you're cute. You'd get a lot of interest I'm sure." He scrolled through thumbnails of selfies. "This time of year is awesome because we get all the tourists too. You just need to get laid, or blown, or something. Then you'll see there are plenty of other fish in the sea and that might make it easier for you to be friends with Cam."

He had a point. Alex's sex life had been on hold for too long, partly because he'd been waiting to have the privacy and freedom of leaving home, and partly because of Cam. But it didn't look like he was going to get either of those things in the near future, so maybe it was time to make that leap.

"I'll think about it." Alex's phone chimed again. It was his dad this time.

Alex, text me please.

"Ugh. Maybe I should tell my parents by message, give them time to calm down before I see them?"

"Sounds like a plan," Amber said. "Get it over with."

Alex typed a message to both his parents: *Got ABD. D*

in Business Studies, so I won't get in to either course now.
He pressed send, feeling sick.

His dad was the first to respond: *I'm coming home for lunch so we can discuss it. Be back by midday.*

It was clearly an order rather than a request, and Alex knew it wouldn't be worth arguing or trying to delay the inevitable. He checked the time. It was eleven now.

Okay, he sent back. Then put his phone away.

"I'm going back to see my parents at lunchtime."

Hayden patted him on the knee. "Sorry, mate."

There wasn't much else to say. Alex picked up his now-empty coffee cup. More caffeine and sugar might help him deal with the confrontation to come. "I fancy another drink. Does anyone else want one?"

ALEX MADE it home a few minutes before twelve. His stomach churned with anxiety as he let himself in.

"Is that you, Alex?" His mum called through from the kitchen.

"Yeah." Reluctantly, he went through to find her pouring a bag of salad into a bowl. The oven was on, and there was a smell of something savoury that would normally have piqued Alex's appetite. Today it made him feel queasy.

His mum glanced up as he came in and the pinched frown on her face spoke before she did. "Your father isn't happy."

No: *I'm sorry love,* or, *Are you okay?*

As was usual in this house, everything was about his father's feelings. This was Alex's problem to deal with but his mum didn't seem to care how he was doing, only how it affected his dad's mood.

"No shit," he said.

"Alex!" Her voice was full of warning. "You'd better tone down that attitude before he gets here."

"Don't worry, Mum. I have no desire to make him more pissed off than he already is."

"He texted me when he left, and he's only coming from Sandy Bay Park, so he'll be here any minute. Lay the table please. The quiche is nearly ready."

Glad for something to occupy him, Alex busied himself getting out placemats, plates, and cutlery while waiting for the sound of his father's key in the door. It was like waiting for the executioner's axe to fall.

When he finally heard the door, he tensed, listening to the heavy tread of his father's feet across the tiled hallway.

"Is he home?" His voice boomed. "He'd better not be late."

"I'm here." Alex straightened up to meet his father's scowl. He squared his shoulders and lifted his chin, trying not to show his fear. It wasn't that his father was violent. He'd never hit Alex, but his temper was vicious, and as a child Alex had been terrified of his shouting, always afraid that one day he would accidentally push him too far.

"What the bloody hell went wrong, Alex?" His father put his hands on his hips and waited for Alex to reply. He was a big man. Tall and broad, with a frame that carried increasing amounts of fat as well as muscle now he was over fifty.

"I don't know," Alex said honestly. "I thought I'd be okay, that I'd done enough revision... but some of the papers didn't go well."

"Obviously," he barked.

"Can we talk about this calmly, Martin?" Alex's mum

said. "Lunch is ready. Let's sit."

Alex's father pulled out his chair at the head of the table with a screech on the tiled floor. "Sure. Let's play happy families, eh, Alex?"

Knowing better than to make some smart retort, Alex sat in his usual seat to the left of his father. Thank goodness it was easy to avoid eye contact in this position.

As his mum carried the quiche and salad to the table, Alex's father asked, "So what are you going to do now? Can you still get into a course to study this year? Your grades weren't terrible overall and there must be places to fill."

"I don't know." He hadn't had the time or mental energy to consider a contingency plan yet. "I'm not sure anywhere will take me to do Business Studies with a D in that subject." His mum slid a slice of quiche onto his plate, and then piled some salad on before serving his father.

"Surely it's worth a try though? If you phone around, somewhere might take you. Your school reports were always good."

It was possible Alex might have been able to find somewhere that would give him a place on a course, but as he thought about it, Alex realised that although he was gutted that he wasn't going to get to leave home, he was also relieved that he didn't have to go and study a subject he found boring.

Bracing himself, he said, "I don't want to do Business Studies anyway. I wasn't interested in it, which is part of the reason I did badly. I think maybe I'd like to do some other A levels, and reapply for a different degree eventually."

"Like what?" His father's voice was eerily calm. He cut a piece of quiche and forked it into his mouth. A crumb escaped and caught on his beard; Alex tried not to stare at it.

"Sociology. I wanted to do that for A level, remember?" Bitterness crept into Alex's voice as he remembered the argument they'd had about that. His father had pushed and pushed until Alex had caved and agreed to go with Business Studies and Economics instead of the Sociology and History that he'd wanted to take."

"Being interested in something doesn't guarantee you earning a living from it," his father said through his mouthful of food, displaying chewed-up quiche that totally put Alex off eating any of his.

"Having a good degree in any academic subject will help me get a job after graduation." Alex kept his voice calm and reasonable.

"Not in this day and age, boy. There are graduates working in every supermarket and coffee shop in the country. Give me one good reason why your mother and I should house, feed, and clothe you for another two years of studying when you messed up this time? Maybe we should chuck you out of the nest. Make you stand on your own two feet at last. When you realise how tough it is out there in the world you might see why I pushed you into a subject that would help you earn a living eventually."

Alex was silent.

His mother's gaze darted anxiously between them. "Come on, Martin, I'm sure we can work something out."

With a flash of inspiration Alex blurted out, "I can get another job, work longer hours, and do online courses. Then I can study and still earn money, so I can pay you rent."

Despite growing up a child of a wealthy father, Alex had always been expected to do chores to earn his allowance. Then once he was fifteen he'd started working part-time at the nearest caravan park his father owned. Now he was eighteen his parents were under no obligation to support him even though they could easily afford to do so. Alex didn't want to be beholden to his father for anything. He would rather pay his own way than have to depend on them when it was clear his father saw him as a burden. And maybe, if he could earn enough, he could eventually move out and rent his own place.

"Mmm." His father looked mollified by this suggestion. "That's not a bad plan. I can give you more hours in the business, maybe get you started on some reception and office work alongside the cleaning. That way you'd be learning some new skills too."

Fuck. The last thing Alex wanted was to do more work for his father, but given the tension of the current situation he didn't dare decline. At least he got paid a decent rate there, so he could probably do a lot worse.

"Okay, thanks."

"Right," his mum said brightly. "That's all settled then. Now eat up, Alex. You haven't touched your lunch."

SEVEN

Cam got a text from Alex around half past three that read: *Can I come to yours for dinner? Can't face another family meal today after lunchtime.*

Sure, Cam replied. *Everything okay?*

It's not the best. But could be worse I guess.

Frowning, Cam wished they could talk properly. He hoped Alex's dad hadn't been too much of an arsehole, but given his personality that seemed unlikely. *I'll text when I leave work and you can come straight round.*

Okay thanks.

As Cam put his phone back in his pocket, he caught his boss watching him. Luckily he hadn't been on his phone too long. Jim, his boss, was pretty relaxed about the occasional text, but if his employees took the piss then he'd pull them up on it. He got back to the shrubs he was planting, redoubling his efforts. If he got this lot finished, Jim might let him go a little early.

Sure enough, when Cam approached Jim an hour later to let him know he was done with the planting, Jim looked over at Cam's work and said, "You've made a nice job of that, well done, mate."

"What do you want me to do now?"

Jim pushed his cap back and scratched his head. "I reckon you can knock off for today. You can get stuck into that other border tomorrow."

"Cheers, boss." Cam grinned. "Have a good evening."

"You too." Jim put his cap back on and touched the brim in a small salute. "See you tomorrow."

CAM TEXTED Alex as he walked to his car.

Leaving work now. Be home in 20 or so.

He was already driving when his phone chimed with a reply. He checked it at a red light to see a smiley face from Alex, along with: *see you soon.*

After a quick pit stop to buy beer, pizzas, and a large tub of ice cream, Cam made it home by five to find Alex waiting on his doorstep.

"Hi, how are you?" Cam asked as he got out of his car.

Alex shrugged. "Been better." He managed a small smile but it wasn't very convincing.

"Come here." Cam pulled him into a hug, realising too late that he was wearing a day's worth of hard-work sweat. "Sorry I probably stink."

"I don't care." Alex squeezed him tighter, his voice muffled by Cam's shoulder.

Sensing Alex needed extra TLC today, Cam waited until Alex started to draw away before releasing him. "Shitty day?" he said.

"The shittiest."

"Will beer, pizza, and ice cream help?"

This time Alex's smile was a little wider. "Yeah, probably."

"Let me get them out of my car then, before the ice cream melts."

Cam let them inside, stopping in the narrow hallway to toe off his rigger boots before leading the way to the kitchen.

"Are you hungry now?" he asked.

"Yeah, starving. I haven't eaten much today."

Cam turned the oven on for the pizzas before putting the ice cream in the freezer, and then he opened them a beer each and handed one to Alex.

"Thanks." Alex took a swig.

After a gulp of his own beer, Cam put his can down so he could put the other beers in the fridge and unwrap the pizzas. "This should probably be pre-heated but whatever." He put them in the oven. Getting out his phone, he set a timer. "I'll give them an extra few minutes. Let's go and sit in the living room." Wicksy didn't usually get home till six so they'd have the place to themselves till then.

Sitting against the armrest of the sofa with his socked feet up, he left space for Alex at the other end. "So tell me about your day. What happened with your parents at lunch?"

"I got summoned home for a talk after I texted them my results," Alex said glumly. "It didn't go well, unsurprisingly."

"So what's happening about uni? Can you still go somewhere different?" Cam had no clue how these things worked.

"I probably could if I wasn't picky. But when I didn't get into the courses I'd applied for, I realised that in some ways I was relieved. I mean... it's shitty that I don't get to leave home, because that was something I was looking forward to. But I never wanted to do Business Studies anyway. I think I'd have hated it and been bored and miserable. So perhaps that's the silver lining? Now I can think about what I really want to do."

"So, what's your plan?"

"I don't know. I haven't had much time to think yet and I need to do some research into courses. But I reckon I might try and do two new A levels online, and reapply to study something completely different."

"Why study online? Couldn't you go to the college in St Austell?"

"My dad doesn't want to support me financially. This way I can work, and pay rent, and still do the A levels."

"Seriously?" Cam was incredulous. "Your dad's not short of a bob or two. What a tight bastard."

Alex shrugged. "He's a self-made man, as he likes to remind me constantly, and he thinks I need to stand on my own two feet," he said that in a deep, gruff voice, imitating his father. "Plus he doesn't approve of the subjects I want to study. He thinks History and Sociology are a waste of time." He took a long swallow of his beer. "Arsehole."

Cam was glad Alex had been the one to say it. He could think of plenty of choice words for Alex's dad, but he didn't think it was his place to be rude about him. He might be a total git but he was still Alex's father. "What about your mum? What did she say about all this?"

"Not a lot, she always sides with him. God forbid she dares to have a different opinion," Alex said. "But at least I'm not homeless, I guess. When I said about working and paying rent—my dad seemed okay with that. He's going to give me more hours working for him."

"Is that what you want?" Cam asked.

Alex snorted. "Not really. But I need to pick my battles. At least it's a reliable job and the pay isn't too bad. If I keep my head down and don't get on the wrong side of him, perhaps I can look out for other jobs and get something else lined up eventually. For now, it'll do."

"What are your friends going to be doing next year? Will any of them still be around?"

"Hayden's still going to be living here. He's going to college in St Austell to do hairdressing." Cam smiled. He could totally see that. Hayden's hair was always perfect, and now he understood why. "But Sophia and Amber are both going to be leaving. They're not going far—Plymouth and Exeter—but realistically, I know they'll only come back at weekends sometimes. I'm happy for them. But...." Alex shrugged. "It's going to be weird not having them around all the time." Alex looked down at his can of beer with a small frown.

Cam wanted to smooth it away. "Is it really selfish of me to say that I'm glad you're not going to be leaving town any time soon?"

He was rewarded when Alex's frown lifted as he raised his gaze to meet Cam's. "A little, maybe." He gave a small grin. "But I'll take it as a compliment, so I think you got away with it."

"It is a compliment. I'd miss you if you left."

Alex's expression turned serious again and he held Cam's gaze. "Yeah," he said softly. "I'd miss you too."

They stared at each other for a drawn-out moment. The shutters had lifted and Alex's longing was suddenly plain to see.

Cam's heart raced. His feelings about Alex were so complicated: affection, attraction, protectiveness. There were so many unspoken words and tangled, conflicting desires fighting for space in his head. Now Alex was staying, it was going to be harder to stick to his resolve to keep things platonic. But with most of Alex's friends moving away he needed Cam's friendship more than ever. Plus with Alex already in a difficult situation with his parents, Cam didn't want to risk making things worse. It wasn't like he had a great track record with relationships. If he got involved with Alex, it probably wouldn't last long and Cam knew from bitter experience that fooling around with friends could sometimes end badly. His heart twisted as he remembered Leanne, one of his best friends from school. A brief summer fling when they were both eighteen had irrevocably ruined their friendship because she'd wanted more than Cam was ready for. He still regretted losing what they'd had before sex complicated things.

The timer on his phone cut through the silence, shattering the tension between them, and giving Cam an excuse to escape. "Pizza!" he said, jumping up. "I'll go and check it."

BY THE TIME they'd eaten the pizza and followed it with ice cream, Wicksy was home. The three of them ended up having a couple more beers and watching some zombie apocalypse film on Netflix. That was a good distraction from any lingering tension between Cam and Alex. It was hard to have romantic swoony feelings about someone while you were watching people being eaten by zombies.

Wicksy was dozing off towards the end of the film. Cam nudged Alex and pointed across to Wicksy on the other side of him. Wicksy's eyes were shut and his head was dropping towards his chest only to jerk up as he fought sleep. He started to slump again; this time listing sideways till his head was resting on Cam's shoulder.

Alex chuckled quietly.

"Get off you eejit." Cam shoved Wicksy's head off him.

"What?" Wicksy sat up, looking confused.

"You're falling asleep on me. Go to bed."

"Mmph." Rubbing his eyes, Wicksy yawned. "Yeah. Probably should. Okay, night, fellas." He heaved himself up and stumbled sleepily out of the living room, looking a bit like one of the zombies in the film.

With Wicksy gone, the mood in the room shifted again. Cam was suddenly overly conscious of Alex sitting close. With three of them on the sofa they'd had to squeeze up. Now, despite the extra space, neither of them moved to make use of it.

"How are you feeling?" Cam asked.

"I'm okay." But Alex didn't meet Cam's gaze and there was a pinched look to his expression that belied his words.

"I don't believe you."

Alex sighed. "Yeah. I guess I'm still feeling pretty crappy."

"I'm sorry." Cam reached for the remote and turned the volume lower. Neither of them was paying much attention to the film now.

"I really wanted to come out. I'm tired of keeping my sexuality a secret; it's stressful and exhausting. I keep thinking that maybe I should do it anyway. Just tell my parents. What's the worst thing that could happen? I mean, they won't like it, but other than disapproving of me what can they actually do? I don't think they'd kick me out, or hurt me or anything. But then I remember what my dad's like and I know I can't risk it. Not while I'm living with him.

I just feel shit about it. I hate having to hide who I am, and it feels as if my entire life is on hold."

Cam's gut feeling was that Alex telling his parents would be a very bad idea indeed. "You need to keep yourself safe, Alex. And there are other, non-physical, ways of hurting someone."

"They're already hurting me." Alex's voice cracked, and Cam glanced sideways to see his eyes were bright with unshed tears.

"Come here." Cam drew him into a hug and Alex went willingly, wrapping his arms tightly around Cam, and pressing his face into Cam's shoulder. Cam remembered he still hadn't showered after work and probably smelt gross, but Alex didn't seem to care.

"Thanks," Alex said, resting in Cam's arms. "I need this."

"Anytime," Cam replied. "Seriously. I'm always here for you. Hang out here as much as you like if being at home with your parents is getting you down."

"What about Wicksy? Would he mind me being here even more often?"

"No, he won't mind at all." Wicksy was easy-going and sociable. Cam was sure he wouldn't mind Alex being there more than he already was.

"Okay, thanks." Alex finally lifted his head from Cam's shoulder and drew back, smiling. "You're a good mate, Cam. I really appreciate it."

They finished the zombie film and started watching a comedy instead. At some point it felt natural for Cam to put an arm around Alex's shoulders and Alex leant in, pressed warm against Cam's side. They'd both been yawning for a while, but Cam didn't want to ask Alex to leave.

Finally, a little after midnight, Alex disentangled himself and stood, stretching. "I'd better go. Thanks for a really nice evening. It cheered me up."

"Like I said, anytime." Cam stood too, and followed Alex into the hallway to see him out.

They hugged again, squeezing each other hard as though reluctant to let go. When they eventually separated, Alex turned away to open the door. Cam felt the loss of him already.

"Night. See you soon." Alex flashed Cam a final smile, and then disappeared into the night.

Cam closed the door behind him and went up to bed alone—as usual. It had been weeks since he'd made any effort to hook up with anyone. He wasn't sure what that meant, and he didn't want to examine it too closely. He was conflicted enough already.

EIGHT

Late September

ALEX LEANT on the reception desk at Sandy Bay Caravan Park and stared out of the window at the rain-washed grey sky. He'd got soaked cycling in to work this morning, but his mum had needed her car to get to Pilates so he hadn't been able to borrow it like he sometimes did. It was hardly worth him being at work today. Now the main tourist season was over, the site was quiet. Only half the vans were inhabited and the rain was keeping everyone indoors. The site reception doubled as a shop that sold basic groceries and provided change for the washing machines and tumble dryers. In peak season on a sunny day there were people in and out all the time, but today Alex had hardly seen a soul.

He wished he'd brought his laptop so he could have got on with some studying. The online Sociology and History courses he'd started were both really interesting and he was in the middle of writing an essay for Sociology. But with the heavy rain earlier he hadn't wanted to risk his laptop getting wet on his morning ride in.

Bored and restless, he got out his phone and read the last message from Cam: *Looking forward to seeing you tomorrow* :)

It made Alex smile. They saw each other nearly every day, but Cam had rugby training tonight. He had said Alex could come over after, but Alex was conscious of how much time he'd spent at Cam's place already and didn't want to push his luck. With Amber and Sophia gone, and Hayden busy with new mates from college—and more recently a boyfriend who took up all his time—Alex was wary of being too dependent on Cam. But it was difficult when their friendship was the one thing that made his life bearable at the moment.

Even that friendship was a double-edged sword.

Alex loved spending time with Cam, but was constantly aware of the nagging feeling that it wasn't enough. Any hopes Alex had of getting over his crush on Cam were futile. The more time they spent together, the harder Alex found it to keep his feelings in check. He had considered raising the subject with Cam again. After all, it was three months since they'd fooled around on the night out after his exams finished. Although Cam had dashed Alex's hopes then for a second time by once again insisting on nothing more than friendship, it was possible that he felt differently now.

Or perhaps any fleeting attraction he'd felt for Alex had waned. If that was the case, Alex would rather not know.

Scrolling through his messages, he found a conversation with Amber from a couple of days ago.

Amber: *Have you joined Grindr yet? Go on, Alex. It's about time you moved on.*

Alex: *Moved on from what?*
Amber: *You know what—or rather, who.*
Alex: *I'll think about it.*
Amber: *That's what you said the last time.*

A rare wave of recklessness swept through Alex, making his heart pound. Maybe it was time to let go of his dream of something happening with Cam. He went to the app store and searched. Recognising the Grindr logo immediately from Hayden's phone, Alex clicked to download.

As soon as it was installed, he opened the app and created an account before he could chicken out and change his mind. Still without a profile photo, he filled in a few basic details—age, height, weight, etc.—and made his profile live.

He went to the grid where he could see other users in the area and started to scroll. Unsurprisingly, there weren't many guys very close, but it was the middle of the day and he knew from Hayden that the app was usually busier in the evening. There were very few men with photos of their faces, but there were lots of torso shots, and several with no image at all—like Alex's. When he realised he was much more likely to take notice of the profiles with photos, he nipped into the office behind the reception desk and shut the door. After stripping off his shirt, Alex took a selfie of his torso up against a blank wall that would give no clues to his exact location. He made sure his jeans were slung low so the waistband of his underwear was showing. Eyeing the photo critically, he decided it would have to do. He was too skinny and too pale, but neither of those were things he could fix easily, so he uploaded the photo and set it as his profile image.

The sound of the bell on the reception desk made him jump guiltily. He pulled his T-shirt back on, shoved his phone in his pocket, and hurried out to find a woman with a couple of kids waiting at the desk.

"Sorry to keep you. How can I help?"

They wanted suggestions for wet weather things to do, so Alex gave her some leaflets for local aquariums, zoos, museums, and soft play centres. "There's also swimming pools, of course. The nearest one is in Bodmin, but there's a more exciting one in Falmouth if you don't mind the longer drive. That one has water slides and a wave machine. It's pretty cool."

"Thanks," the woman said with a smile.

Just then Alex's phone chimed with an alert that he recognised from Hayden's phone as a Grindr notification. He flushed, saying, "You're welcome. Hope you have a good day."

As soon as she and the kids were gone, he got his phone out and his heart leapt with nerves and excitement when he saw he had a message from someone called BBoo.

All it said was, *Hey*. But at least it was a start.

Checking out BBoo's profile, Alex saw a torso shot that was remarkably similar to his own other than the fact that this guy had a tan. His age said eighteen, height six feet, weight one hundred and forty-five pounds. With a rush of adrenaline, Alex noticed that he was only four hundred metres away.

Hi, how's it going? Alex replied.

Not bad. Bored though.

Me too.

What are you doing? BBoo asked.

Not a lot, Alex sent back. He didn't want to say he was working. That was too much of a clue to his identity if this guy was staying at Sandy Bay, as Alex suspected. They might have already seen each other around. *How about you?*

On holiday with my parents and sister, and stuck inside cus of the rain. Guess it beats being in double Chemistry tho.

It seemed like a weird time of year for a teenager to be away with his parents. But some families took their kids out of school for a week to take advantage of the cheaper off-peak rates.

You're still at school then? Alex asked.

Yeah. Final year.

Alex was trying to decide what to ask next, but BBoo beat him to it: *I'm horny. You wanna hook up and blow each other or something?*

Heat rushed through Alex at the thought of getting off with some random stranger. It would feel so dirty—in a good way, Alex hoped. And it had been way too long since he'd done anything with another person. Apart from that humiliating hand job with Cam, Hayden was the last, and that had been over a year ago.

Maybe, but can I see your face first? I'm Alex BTW. Beggars couldn't be choosers, but Alex wanted to make sure he was at least slightly attracted to BBoo before he committed to anything.

Sure, Alex. I'm Ben, and I'd like to see you too.

Ben followed up with a photo. He was pretty cute. Not Cam levels of hotness, but no guy could measure up in Alex's mind. Ben had dark, messy-looking hair, and a nice smile. He was ordinary, but in some ways that was good because it made him less intimidating.

Thanks :)

Alex took a quick selfie and sent that too, really hoping it wouldn't put Ben off.

You're cute, Ben replied. *So... what do you reckon? Want to meet and see what happens?*

Alex's heart thumped hard as he considered it.

Yeah. It was about time he accepted that nothing was ever going to happen with Cam. A quick hook-up with Ben might be just the boost he needed for his confidence in order to be able to move on.

Yeah. Okay. Alex let his finger hover over the screen for a moment before finally hitting send.

You free now?

No. But I have a lunch break at 12. That was less than an hour away. At this time of year nobody covered Alex's breaks, but he was allowed to leave the desk if he wanted. Normally he didn't bother as there was nothing else to do there anyway.

Where can we meet?

Alex hadn't even thought about that. He could hardly take Ben back to his house. Although his dad was normally out all day, his mum was often at home so that was way too risky. Presumably Ben had no privacy if he was stuck in a static caravan with his family. The toilet block? At least they could lock themselves in a cubicle. But no. Alex thought he'd be too nervous about being busted to be able to even get it up, let alone come. Outdoors somewhere? There were secluded spots in the woods by the coast path, but you never knew when you might get surprised by a random dog walker. Plus it was still pissing down with rain and it looked likely to persist for the rest of the day.

Suddenly Alex had a flash of inspiration. There were two rows of older caravans that were due to be refurbished over the winter. Tucked away on the far side of the site, they were all empty at the moment, and Alex had access to the keys.

Van number 70, meet me there just after 12.

Okay :)

The phone rang then.

When Alex had finished talking to someone who wanted to book a van for school half-term in October, he opened Grindr again and re-read the messages. He decided to let the conversation drop for now. He'd be able to talk to Ben in person soon enough.

At twelve, Alex put up a sign on the reception desk that read: *Closed for lunch, back at 1pm*. He stopped at the toilet block on his way and had a piss in one of the urinals. Relieved that nobody else was there, he gave his dick a quick wash in the sink. It seemed only polite to try to be clean if someone might be about to suck it for him. The thought of that had him stiffening up in his hand as he tucked himself away. After that, he rinsed his mouth out, wishing he could brush his teeth.

Hoodie pulled up against the rain, Alex hurried to the edge of the site where the older vans were. As he turned into the row for the vans numbered seventy to seventy-nine he saw another hooded figure leaning against seventy.

Heart thumping with nerves and excitement, Alex approached, and Ben looked up and smiled.

"Hi," Alex said, a little breathless from rushing.

"Hey, Alex. Good to meet you." Ben stuck out a hand and Alex took it and shook. He gave an awkward chuckle. "This is very formal."

"Yeah, sorry," Ben said. "I'm really nervous. Not really sure what the etiquette is. I haven't done this much."

Relieved that Ben seemed genuine, Alex relaxed. "Me neither." He got out the key to the van. "Shall we get out of the rain?"

"Yes please."

The lock was a little stiff, but Alex managed to turn the key after a bit of wiggling. Inside the van was dark and gloomy. The curtains were drawn and blocked most of the daylight. It smelt a little damp.

"Are you not staying here then?" Ben asked, looking around at the obviously uninhabited van with a frown of confusion.

"No. I work here." Alex grinned. "I knew this whole row was empty, so it seemed like a good place to meet."

"Awesome."

They were standing just inside the door, facing each other. Alex let his gaze take in Ben properly. He was as cute in person as he was in his photo. He'd put his hood down, and his hair was messy and cool. He was wearing blue board shorts and a dark-grey hoodie. His grin was mischievous and Alex felt a flicker of arousal start to build as he imagined what they might do together.

"Shall we sit down?" Alex suggested.

"Okay." The van had seating all around the far end of the living space that extended further along one wall. They took a seat on the part that wasn't around the table. "What do you want to do?" Ben shuffled closer to Alex, closing the gap so their thighs touched.

"We could start with kissing?" Feeling daring, Alex put his hand on Ben's leg. He felt firm muscle under the fabric of his shorts.

"Sounds like a plan." Smiling, Ben leant in, and Alex met him halfway in a tentative press of lips.

It felt like ages since Alex had done this. He'd forgotten how strange it was, the peculiar intimacy of having your mouth on someone else's. Ben put his hand on Alex's cheek and kept him there, deepening the kiss in a way that made heat flush through Alex's body, pooling in his groin with the warm weight of arousal.

Kissing him back, Alex was gratified when Ben made an

appreciative sound. He felt Ben's other hand on his thigh, sliding upwards slowly. When Ben's hand reached the bulge in Alex's shorts, Alex couldn't hold back a moan as he squeezed gently.

Alex returned the favour, seeking out Ben's dick, and rubbing it. Ben was as hard as he was, and that turned Alex on even more. Made bold by desire, Alex broke the kiss and muttered, "Can I suck you?"

"Oh God, yes please," Ben replied breathlessly. "Then I'll blow you after."

Moving onto his knees between Ben's spread thighs; Alex helped Ben tug his board shorts down. He had a nice cock: straight, uncut, and pointing eagerly upwards from a thatch of bushy dark pubes. The scent of masculine arousal made Alex's mouth water as he lowered his mouth and tentatively sucked on the head.

"Fuck." Ben groaned, putting his hands on Alex's head and threading his fingers into his hair. "That feels awesome."

Alex sucked harder, deeper, remembering all the things he'd learnt with Hayden. Hayden had been a good coach, telling Alex what felt good, and Alex remembered what he'd liked when Hayden had done this to him. He tried all those things now, sucking, stroking with his tongue, using his hand along with his mouth. Desperate for stimulation, he undid his fly, and squeezed his cock, resisting the urge to stroke it in earnest, afraid that he'd come in his pants if he did.

Ben was very vocal, cursing and moaning as Alex focused on making him feel good.

Perhaps if Ben had been quieter, Alex would have heard the sounds of voices outside, but as it was he was pulled abruptly out of the moment by the sound of the van door opening behind him, electric light flooding the dim interior, and his father's voice saying, "So, as you can see it needs some—"

Frozen with horror, Alex couldn't move.

"Shit!" Ben shoved Alex's head away, covering himself with his hands, and scrabbling desperately to pull up his shorts.

"What the bloody hell is going on in here?" Alex's father shouted, his voice furious and blustering. "This is private property. You perverts have no right to be here. I'm calling the police right now."

"No!" Alex jumped to his feet, fumbling with his fly, and turned to see his father with his phone in his hand. "Don't. I'm sorry." Two other men flanked him, but Alex focused on his father, watching in horrified fascination as his face turned from an angry red to the pallor of shock.

"Alex!" He shook his head. "What...?"

Dizzy with panic and nausea, Alex wondered if it was possible to have a heart attack at the age of eighteen. "I'm sorry, Dad," he said quietly. He wasn't sure exactly what he was apologising for. The misuse of the van? Having his father finding out this way? He wasn't apologising for being gay; that wasn't something he could help.

"Oh fuck. This is your dad?" Ben's shocked voice reminded Alex that he was still there.

"Yep."

"I should go." Ben stood, clothes back in place now. He glanced nervously at Alex's father and then back at Alex. "You gonna be okay?"

"Yeah." Alex has no clue whether he was going to be okay, but it wasn't Ben's problem. The poor guy looked as though he was about to shit himself.

Alex could identify with that.

Ben hurried towards the door, skirting around the three men who blocked his path. The other men watched him go, but Alex's father ignored him completely, his attention focused entirely on Alex.

One of the men cleared his throat. "Shall we leave you to it, Mr Elliot?" He rubbed the back of his neck, clearly uncomfortable. "Seems like you have a bit of a, um... family situation to deal with here. We can come back later, or tomorrow."

"Later will be fine. Give me an hour." His voice was as cold as the gaze he had fixed on Alex. Stomach lurching with fear, Alex squared his shoulders as the other two men left, and the door clicked shut behind them.

Once they were gone, the silence was unbearable. Alex waited, the seconds ticking past until he couldn't stand it anymore.

"I'm sorry," he said again.

"So you fucking should be." His father's icy tone terrified Alex more than his usual blustering anger. This was new, and Alex didn't know what it meant. He tried not to cower as his father walked towards him, closing the gap until Alex could smell the sourness of stale coffee on his breath and see the hairs in his nostrils. "How fucking *dare* you?" he hissed. The controlled rage a measured attack, his words like guided missiles homing in on a helpless target. "You disgusting little faggot. Getting on your knees for another boy on my property, right under my nose. You make me *sick*." He moved so fast, Alex barely had time to register before his dad's hand made contact with a blow to Alex's face that whipped his head back, sharp pain blooming as he stumbled and fell. Then yet more pain as his back made contact with the edge of the seat.

Instinctively, Alex curled into a ball, ready to shield

himself from more blows, but none came. He uncovered his face in time to see his father's expression of pure disgust as he spat on Alex where he lay on the floor. "Now fuck off. Get off my property. I can't bear to look at you."

Moving on autopilot, Alex's limbs felt disconnected and clumsy as he scrambled to his feet and ran past him. Face burning from where he'd been struck, and back aching from where he'd landed, he ignored the pain. He needed to get away, as far away as he could from this person he barely recognised. Looking at that face twisted with cruelty and hatred, Alex could no longer think of that man as his father.

The rain mingled with hot tears that streaked his cheeks as he ran to where his bike was locked. His helmet was in the site office and so was his raincoat but he didn't stop to get them. He unlocked his bike with trembling fingers, threw himself onto it, and pedalled away as fast as he could, heading instinctively for the one place he knew he'd be safe.

NINE

Cam's phone rang, but he ignored it. Busy doing some maintenance work on one of the ride-on lawnmowers at work—always a good job to do on a rainy day—he let it go to voicemail.

It rang again immediately.

With a huff of annoyance, he wiped his oily hands on a rag, and got his phone out a second too late to answer the call.

It was from an unknown number so he didn't bother to call back, assuming it would be some annoying sales or insurance thing, but then it rang yet again.

"Who is this?" he snapped.

"Cam? It's Seb—from Rainbow Place."

"Oh, Seb. Hi. What's up?" Cam couldn't think why on earth Seb might be calling him. They knew each other a little because Cam was a regular customer, but they weren't what you'd call close friends, so this was quite out of the blue.

"I've got Alex here." Something in Seb's tone instantly had Cam on alert.

"What is it? What's wrong?"

"He had a run in with his father. Things turned pretty nasty and he's not in a good way—emotionally more than physically," he added quickly. "He asked me to call you and see if you can come."

Cam was already moving in the direction of Jim's office. Luckily on a rainy day he was pretty dispensable; they always struggled to fill the time when it was too wet to be working outdoors. "I'll be there as soon as I can. Tell Alex I'm on my way."

He knocked on Jim's door as a formality; it was ajar anyway so he pushed it open.

"Alright." Jim glanced up from his desk. He looked all wrong behind a computer, his weather-beaten face frowning behind glasses he didn't need for outdoor work. "What's up?"

"There's an emergency with a mate of mine. I need to leave if that's okay?"

Jim frowned in concern. "Of course, lad. We can do without you for the rest of the day."

"Thanks. I'll make the time up, or you can knock it off my wages this week."

"There's no need. You wouldn't be doing much this afternoon anyhow, don't worry about it. Now go, see your mate. I hope he's okay."

Cam hoped so too, but it didn't sound good.

All sorts of horrible scenarios ran through his head as he drove down into Porthladock. What on earth had happened between Alex and his dad?

CAM BURST through the doors of Rainbow Place, looking for Alex or Seb but there was no sign of either of them.

Worried, he went to the counter, bypassing a few people who were queuing. "Sorry, excuse me," he called to the twenty-something guy behind the bar who was on the till taking orders. He was new here and Cam didn't know his name. "I'm looking for Seb and Alex, are they here?"

"They're in the kitchen," the guy replied. "Are you Cam?" Cam nodded. "Just go through. They're expecting you." He smiled, dimples showing through reddish-blond stubble.

"Cheers."

Pushing open the kitchen door, Cam found Alex and Seb tucked away in a corner on two chairs that had been brought through from the main room. Amelia, one of the chefs, and Tom, a kitchen assistant, were bustling around getting on with their work. They both greeted Cam quietly as he passed, but all his attention was on Alex. Seb had an arm around him, and Alex was holding an ice pack against his cheek. They both looked up as Cam approached and Alex let the ice pack drop.

"Cam." Alex's voice cracked as he stood to greet him.

There was a vivid red mark on Alex's cheek, and a bruise already darkening around his eye. Cam's gut lurched with nausea and rage, but he tamped it down so he could give Alex the comfort he so clearly needed. As he opened his arms, Alex burrowed into them, clinging tightly as his body shook with sobs. Desperate to know what had happened, it was obvious that Alex was in no fit state to talk to him yet. So Cam held him close, stroking his back, and murmuring meaningless words of comfort. "It's okay.... It'll be okay."

Seb caught Cam's eye over Alex's shoulder and shook his head, face grim. He stood and patted Cam on the arm. "I'm sorry. I need to get back out there to help Dylan. He's

been holding the fort alone for the last hour. Have a seat."
He gestured to the chairs.

Cam guided Alex down, keeping an arm around him as
Alex sniffed. "Sorry."

"You have *nothing* to be sorry for." Alex seemed calmer
now, so Cam asked cautiously, "Can you tell me what
happened?"

Alex lifted the ice pack to his cheek again, and looked
down at his feet. "My father caught me with a guy. He went
ballistic."

The hot rush of jealousy that flooded through Cam
was totally inappropriate, but he couldn't control it. Trying
not to show how bothered he was by the thought of Alex
with someone else, he asked, "What guy? What
happened?"

"Just some guy I met through Grindr," Alex said, his
cheeks pink. "It was the first time I ever used the app. He
was staying at Sandy Bay and I arranged to meet him in one
of the empty vans due for refurbishment, but my dad
showed up with some blokes who are going to be working
on the vans. I didn't hear him coming, he caught us right in
the middle of... stuff."

"Oh." Cam's brain was immediately filled with images
of the stuff Alex might have been doing with this random
guy. He pushed those thoughts away. Alex needed him to
be supportive, not act like a possessive twat when he had no
right to feel like that anyway. Alex was free to do whatever
he liked with other guys.

"It was awful, Cam. I was on my knees sucking Ben's
dick. Of all the ways for my dad to find out. Jesus!"

"So what did your dad do? And why didn't any of the
others try and stop him?"

"They'd gone. He seemed calm at first—like, obviously

angry, but not out of control. It wasn't till they left that he flipped his lid and hit me."

"How badly are you hurt? Do you need to see a doctor? Let me see." Cam gently turned Alex's face towards him and moved the ice pack so he could see. There was a small cut on Alex's cheekbone, and a bit of swelling. The bruise around his eye was going to be spectacular when it came out properly. Knowing that Alex's father had done this to him made Cam want to hunt him down and beat him senseless.

Fucking arsehole.

"No." Alex shook his head. "It's just a bruise. I hurt my back a bit when I fell, but it's not serious."

"You should report him to the police," Cam said. "He shouldn't get away with this."

"That's what Seb said. But no. I don't want to have to go through what happened with the police, or in court. It's humiliating. I want to try to forget it ever happened."

"But what are you going to do, Alex? You live with him —or you did. Surely you can't go back home now even if you wanted to?"

"I don't know, Cam. I don't know what the fuck to do." Alex's voice was hoarse and strained. "I don't want anything to do with him, but I haven't got anywhere else to go. Maybe last year I could have stayed with Amber, her mum has a spare room, but Amber's away in Plymouth now, and it would be weird being at her house without her even if her mum let me stay for a while. And shit, I don't even have a job now. I can't work for my dad anymore. If I can get another job then maybe I can find somewhere to rent eventually, but in the short term I've got no money. God, it's all so fucking complicated and overwhelming."

"You can stay with me," Cam said. "I don't want you going back under your father's roof. My place isn't ideal, but you can sleep on the sofa. It's yours as long as you need it while you work out what to do. You won't have much privacy, or space to store your stuff, but you'll be safe, and that's the most important thing."

"Seriously? Are you sure?" Alex met Cam's gaze, expression intense.

"Absolutely."

"What about Wicksy?"

"I'm sure he won't mind. But I can call him now to check—if you want to stay with us?"

Nodding, Alex said quietly, "Yes please. I can't think of anywhere else I'd rather be." As Cam pulled out his phone to make the call, Alex said, "Oh shit, I need to reply to Ben. He messaged me earlier asking if I was okay and I forgot to reply." He got out his phone too and opened Grindr. "God, and I have messages from three other guys. Well they're out of luck. After today I'm not really in the mood to hook up." Cam tried not to feel glad about this as Alex deleted the other messages without replying to them. "I think I'm going to delete the app once I've spoken to Ben." He started to type.

"My signal is weak in here, so I'm gonna nip outside to call Wicksy, okay?"

"Sure." Alex looked up and smiled. It was the first genuine smile Cam had seen from him today, it was a relief to see him looking hopeful rather than utterly broken.

AS CAM HAD EXPECTED, Wicksy was totally cool with Alex staying, especially when he explained what had happened with Alex's dad.

"That fucking lowlife," Wicksy raged. "We should send the rugby team round to scare the crap out of him."

"I wish," Cam said. "But at least Alex will be safe at ours. He's probably gonna need some of his stuff though, so maybe you can come with us as backup while he packs."

"Good idea. Sign me up for that."

Cam grinned at his enthusiasm. "Cheers, mate. I'll see you later. Oh... can you send my apologies to Drew, but I won't make training tonight."

"Yeah, of course. Bye."

Cam went back into Rainbow Place. As he passed the bar, Seb called him over. "How's he doing?"

Shrugging, Cam said, "Hard to tell. He's calmer now, but is trying to work out what to do. He doesn't want to go back home."

"I don't blame him, and he shouldn't, not after what happened. I wish he'd involve the police, but we have to respect his decision on that." Seb frowned. "If he needs somewhere to stay, tell him he can have my spare room. I have the space."

"I think he's planning on staying with me for a while, but I only have a sofa in my living room, so I'll let him know you have a better offer."

"Whatever he wants. I wish I could do more to help."

With a flash of inspiration, Cam said, "I think he could use a new job. Have you got any shifts going here? He was working for his dad so he needs something else."

Seb's face lit up. "Yes! I was actually thinking about taking on more staff. We've been stretched since we're getting busier. I might not be able to give him full-time hours but I can definitely give him a few shifts a week, especially if he's happy to work in the kitchen as well as serving. He can take up the slack at our busier times."

"Cool. I'll tell him. Thanks, Seb."

Cam returned to the kitchen to find Alex busy chopping peppers. "Amelia gave me a job to do." He smiled at Cam. "I'm making myself useful instead of getting under everyone's feet."

"Better get used to it," Cam said with a grin, "because Seb has a job for you here if you want it."

"Really?" Alex's smile widened. "He said that?"

"Yeah. He could use some extra help. Oh, and he also offered you his spare room if you need somewhere to stay."

"Wow. That's kind of him. Do you think I should accept? Would that be better for you and Wicksy?"

"It's up to you." Cam didn't want to try to talk Alex into anything. "Wicksy's totally happy for you to stay, and obviously so am I. But if you'd rather have your own room, then Seb's place might be a better option, so maybe you should consider it."

Alex went back to chopping the peppers, a thoughtful frown on his face. "Yeah. I'll think about it. But can I stay at yours tonight at least?"

"Of course." Cam wanted Alex under his roof where he'd know he was safe. Not that he wouldn't be safe with Seb, but Seb didn't know Alex like he did. Cam wanted to be there for him if Alex needed him. Who knew how he'd be feeling in the aftermath of what happened with his dad. "Stay at mine for a few days while you decide what you want to do more long-term."

"Okay. Thanks."

THAT EVENING, Cam, Alex, and Wicksy sat watching some science thing on TV. Alex was already in Cam's sleeping bag wearing one of Cam's old T-shirts that he'd borrowed to sleep in. He'd been yawning, but insisted he wasn't ready to sleep yet. Cam was sitting on the sofa with Alex's feet in his lap, and Wicksy was on the armchair.

They'd bought him a toothbrush from the chemist in town earlier, and Wicksy had the same type of phone charger that Alex used, so he had everything he needed for one night.

Alex's phone rang and as he moved to pick it up he hesitated for a moment. "It's my mum." He looked at Cam, eyes wide. "Do you think she knows what happened?" It obviously wasn't a question Cam could answer. Alex reached for the phone and answered it. "Hi."

He was silent for a moment, and then said, "No. I'm not coming home."

More silence, and Alex's face took on a pinched look. "So he didn't tell you anything about what happened today?" Another pause. "Well, I'm sorry you were worried. I don't want to talk about it now, but if you want to know why I'm not coming home tonight, or for the foreseeable future, then you'd better ask Dad." He pulled the phone away from his ear, ignoring the tinny voice that was still talking as he ended the call. Blowing out a long breath, he said, "Of course I'm gonna have to go home sometime soon to get my stuff, aren't I?"

"We'll come with you," Wicksy said. "So don't you worry about that."

"Thank you." Alex gave him a small smile. "Seriously, thank you both so much."

When the science show finished, Wicksy stood and stretched. "I'm off to bed. Night, guys."

"Night," Alex said.

"Sleep well," Cam added.

Once he was gone, Cam turned the TV off, and

squeezed Alex's feet through the sleeping bag. "How are you feeling?"

"I'm not sure, honestly." Alex frowned, touching the bruises on his face. "It all feels a bit unreal. I still can't believe it happened."

"Yeah. It's a lot to process."

"I should let you get to bed," Alex said. "You've got work in the morning, and I told Seb I'd come down to Rainbow Place to talk about what hours he can offer me."

"You sure? I can keep you company if you want to stay up a bit longer."

"No. I'll be fine. I think I'll be able to sleep soon, and if not I can watch TV. I'll keep the sound down low. Let me just go and brush my teeth, and then I'll try and settle down for the night."

"Okay."

Alex extracted himself from the sleeping bag, and Cam tried not to stare at his arse in the grey boxer briefs he was wearing. As Alex stretched and yawned, the T-shirt of Cam's he was wearing rode up to show lean hips and a line of hair on his belly. Cam allowed himself a quick glance at the bulge in his underwear before tearing his eyes away.

He followed Alex out of the living room and went into his bedroom while Alex used the bathroom. After stripping down to his boxer briefs, Cam was about to put on a different T-shirt to sleep in when there was a tap on his door, which he'd left ajar. "Yeah?" he said quietly.

Alex pushed it open. His gaze flickered over Cam's torso and lower still before making it back up to Cam's face. Cheeks flushing, he said, "I'm done in the bathroom."

"Cool, cheers."

Hesitating in the doorway, Alex held Cam's gaze. Feeling exposed, Cam pulled his T-shirt over his head, breaking their connection for a moment. When he emerged, Alex had moved a little closer. "Thank you so much. For everything. For being my friend, for letting me stay, for leaving work to support me today."

Cam's heart thumped harder and he smiled. "It's nothing. I'm glad I can help."

There was a few beats pause, before Alex asked tentatively, "Can I have a hug?"

"Always." Cam opened his arms, moving forward to meet Alex.

They wrapped their arms around each other, and Cam was surprised by Alex's strength as he held Cam. With their bodies pressed close together, Cam could feel the soft bulge of Alex's junk nestling below his, and he willed his body not to react.

Alex was the one to pull away first, and Cam let him go, half-relieved, but missing the contact already. "Goodnight, Cam," Alex said.

"Night. Sweet dreams."

"You too." Alex grinned before turning and leaving Cam to his frustration.

Alex had moved on, if his earlier adventures with this Ben guy were any indication. So why was Cam still mooning around Alex like a lovesick teenager when he'd been the one to insist they were just friends in the first place? With Alex living under the same roof, he needed to get a handle on his feelings or things could get awkward.

TEN

Alex left the house just before nine the next morning. Cam and Wicksy were both up and about at seven, and although they'd tried to be quiet, the walls in their house were pretty thin. Alex was happy to get up early anyway; the sofa wasn't the most comfortable thing to sleep on.

As he walked down the hill into town, Alex felt self-conscious about the marks on his face as he noticed a few people staring. He held his head high, refusing to act like a victim. He had nothing to be ashamed of. It wasn't his fault his father was a homophobic wanker.

"Good morning, Alex." Seb greeted him with a hug as he arrived at the café, and Dylan gave him a cheery wave from behind the counter.

Walking into Rainbow Place was like being wrapped up in a warm comfort blanket. It was so familiar to Alex now, and he loved it for being somewhere he'd been able to be himself back when only his best friends knew he was queer. The first time he'd come here and connected with other LGBT people and their allies, it had given him hope for the future.

He felt that strength bolstering him again this morning. Even though the shit had hit the fan with his parents, and on paper his life was pretty fucked up at the moment, Alex trusted that better things were coming. At least there was nothing to stop him being out and proud now. The secret he'd guarded so fearfully for so long had been revealed—not in a way Alex would ever have chosen, but there was still some relief in it being out in the open. It was one less thing for him to worry about, even though his father's reaction had given him some new challenges to face: like starting a new job, and working out where he was going to live until he was ready to apply for uni again.

"Can I get you a coffee or tea?" Seb asked. "Then we can sit and have a chat about you working here."

"I'd love a coffee please—a cinnamon latte."

"Actually, why don't you come and help me make it? Learning to use the coffee machine will be one of the key parts of your training."

Once Alex had made his first two coffees, they sat at a quiet corner table and Seb opened his laptop to look at his staff roster. "So, are you happy to do kitchen work as well as serving?"

"I'll do anything you need me to do," Alex said. "Seriously. I'm so grateful to you for offering me a job. I'll do whatever you need."

"Okay." Seb scrolled, frowning in concentration. He picked up a pen and made a few notes on a pad beside him. "Well, I'm not sure if it's enough, but I can offer you four shifts a week. Two in the kitchen, and two serving. They won't be fixed because we have a rota, but they're likely to include quite a lot of weekends because those are our busiest times. Is that okay with you? It's twenty-eight hours in total and the rate of pay is seven quid an hour."

"Yes, that's absolutely fine," Alex said. He quickly did some mental arithmetic, that would be just under two hundred pounds a week. That was a little less than he'd been earning working for his dad, but it would do for now. He'd been paying forty quid a week to his parents for food and bills, and he could afford to offer that to Cam and Wicksy if he was going to stay there for a while. If he wanted to earn enough for rent on his own room somewhere eventually he'd need more hours, or to find a second job, but there was no rush. "Thanks so much, Seb. You're a life saver."

Seb grinned. "It's nothing. You're doing me a favour because I needed someone, and now I don't have to advertise or interview. I know you, I like you, and I'm happy to have you working for me." He closed his laptop and took a sip of his coffee, and then said, "Did Cam tell you that I also offered you a room if you need one? You don't have to pay me rent, I have a spare room and it seems daft for it to be empty when you need somewhere. You're welcome to live there while you get back on your feet. At the moment it's just me in the house—although Jason is probably going to be moving in at the end of the year—so I'm rattling around when he's not staying over, and would be happy to have some company."

"That's so incredibly kind of you." Alex's eyes prickled as a warm rush of emotion swept through him. He knew it made sense to accept; it was daft to sleep on Cam's sofa when Seb was offering him a whole room. But something stopped Alex from saying yes. "Can I think about it? I'm staying with Cam and Wicksy for now, so I'm not totally homeless."

"Of course." Seb's eyes were kind as he studied Alex. "I know you and Cam are close. I can see why you'd want to be with him, especially after what happened yesterday."

Alex felt his cheeks heat. He cast his eyes down, swirling the coffee in his cup. "Yeah. He's a good mate."

"I did wonder if he might be more than a mate," Seb said gently. "I know it's not my business, but it seems like there's something there perhaps?"

"No." Alex shook his head, ignoring the familiar gut punch of disappointment as he added, "No, we're just friends."

Seb frowned. "Oh. Okay, sorry if I overstepped."

"It's fine." Alex managed a smile. "And thanks again for the offer of the room. I may still take you up on it. So, when do you want me to start work?"

"Are you free for the rest of the day today?" Seb asked. "If you are, hang around, and we'll train you. I'll pay you for the hours you stay. It's quiet, so it'll be a good day to learn the ropes."

"Yeah. I have no plans." With Cam at work and Hayden at college, Alex had nothing else to do and he was keen to get started. Speaking of Hayden, he ought to message him and let him know what happened. He'd do that later.

"Perfect. In that case, let me go through the coffee machine with you again, and I'll show you how the till works. Then closer to lunchtime I'm sure Luca will have some jobs for you in the kitchen."

ONCE THE LUNCHTIME rush was over, Alex's head was reeling with new information as he got to grips with all the systems in the café. Being put on kitchen duty was a relief after dealing with coffee orders for a very busy hour. He was quite enjoying the mindless task of peeling and chopping vegetables ready for the evening diners. Luca reminded Alex of a TV chef. He had the looks, the charisma, and the forceful personality, although fortunately he was rather more genial than Gordon Ramsey. Any cursing—which sounded quite romantic in Italian anyway—was directed at himself or the thing he was cooking rather than at Alex or Tom, the other kitchen assistant.

"Do you want to take your break now?" Tom asked Alex. "Or shall I go first?"

"Oh. I don't mind." Alex shrugged, not pausing in his carrot peeling. Absorbed in all the things he had to take in, he hadn't even noticed that he hadn't had a lunch break yet. But with lunch being the busiest time, it made sense that they had their breaks before or after.

"Well I'm starving so I'll nip out now if it's okay with you."

"Yes, sure." Alex was hungry now he'd thought about it, but he didn't mind waiting.

"Cheers." Tom took off his apron and the cap that covered his hair while he was working. He ruffled it with his hands, trying to fix his hat-hair. "That better?" He raised his eyebrows in question.

"Yeah, looks fine." Tom's hair was short and spiky and had recovered quickly from being flattened.

"Cool, see you in a bit then." He gave Alex a cheery grin and a wave as he left.

As Alex carried on working his way through the mountain of vegetables, his phone rang. He got it out to see that it was his dad calling. His stomach lurched and he stared at the screen, trying to decide what to do.

"You can answer if you want," Luca said from the vat of soup he was stirring. "The vegetables can wait."

"Thanks. But it's my father and I'm not that desperate

to speak to him, to be honest." Alex tried to make it sound like a joke, but his voice came out tight and strained.

Luca's expression softened and his gaze flickered to Alex's bruises. "I can imagine."

The phone fell silent and Alex shoved it back in his pocket. "I'll call him when I take my break." The last thing Alex wanted to do was speak to his father, but at some point Alex was going to have to face him, and maybe it would be better to get it over with. If nothing else, he wanted to go home and get his stuff with Cam and Wicksy tonight, and it would be better to know what to expect if his parents were going to be in.

WHEN IT WAS Alex's turn for a break, he went and bought a sandwich and a can of Coke. Then, deciding to get the phone call over with before he ate, he sat on one of the benches by the harbour, pulled up his dad's mobile number, and hit call. He took a deep breath as it rang, willing himself to stay calm and assertive.

"Alex," his father said sharply when he answered. "Where are you? Your mother's been worried."

"Did you tell her why I didn't come home?"

There was a pause and he could hear the rasp of his father's breathing. "I explained we'd had a disagreement."

Alex snorted. "Is that what you'd call it? I'd call it assault." His voice came out hard and strong and he was proud of himself for managing to sound confident when his hands were trembling and his heart was beating so hard he felt dizzy. "I think the police would agree with me."

"Oh come now," his father said, using the genial tone Alex had overheard so many times when he was talking to his political connections. But there was an edge of anxiety to it that told Alex he was rattled. "I may have overreacted, and I apologise for that, but I'm sure we can resolve things without involving the police."

Changing the subject while he had the upper hand, Alex said, "I'm going to come to the house tonight—"

"Good idea. Come home, and then we can talk about this rationally."

"No. I don't want to talk to you. I'm coming to collect my things. I have no intention of spending another night under your roof."

Another pause and the breathing was faster now.

"But where are you going? And what about your job? You didn't turn up today. Will you be back?" His father fired the questions at him in quick succession.

"It's none of your business where I'm going, and you can stick your job. I've found a better one."

"What? Where?"

"Again, it's none of your business. I'll be round this evening with some friends to pack up my stuff. I have to go now. Goodbye."

"But, Alex—"

Alex ended the call with a grim smile of satisfaction on his face.

PAUSING on the doorstep of his parents' house, Alex whispered to Cam. "Should I ring the bell? Or use my keys to open it?"

Cam shrugged. "Whatever feels right."

With Cam and Wicksy flanking him like bodyguards, Alex reckoned he'd make more of an impression by ringing the doorbell and waiting to be let in. This house no longer felt like home, and he couldn't imagine it would ever feel like his home again.

He pressed the bell and they waited.

When Alex heard the sound of someone approaching he braced himself, squaring his shoulders, and lifting his chin.

"Oh, Alex." His mother answered the door looking surprised and relieved. "Did you forget your key?" She glanced at Cam and Wicksy, giving them both a nervous smile.

"No."

She frowned, studying his black eye. "What happened to you?" Her gaze flickered down to the cut on his cheek.

"I believe Dad told you we had a disagreement? Well, that's a bit of an understatement."

Her mouth dropped open in shock and her face paled. "He did that?" she whispered.

Alex nodded.

She stared at him. "Why?"

Holding her gaze unflinchingly, Alex said, "Because he found out I'm gay."

She gasped, hand coming up to cover her mouth. Alex wondered whether she was more shocked by his admission of his sexuality, or by what his father had done in response to it.

"I'm sure he didn't mean to... it must have been a shock. It's a lot to take in...." Her voice trailed off as though she realised how pathetic her half-baked excuses were.

"This wasn't an accident, Mum," Alex said coldly. "It was deliberate. He verbally abused me, and then he punched me in the face, and knocked me down. It was completely unprovoked."

"I know he has a temper, but I don't think—"

"I'm not interested in hearing you justify his behaviour. We're only here to get my stuff. Can we come in?"

"Of course, Alex. This is your home." She stood aside to let them pass.

"Not anymore it isn't. Once I've got my things I'm not coming back."

The door to his father's study opened, "What's going on out here, Sylvia?" Alex's father hurried out into the hall and stopped short when he saw Alex and his friends. "Oh. It's you." Alex's mum scurried to stand beside his father in another plain display of her allegiance.

"Yes. I was just explaining our *disagreement* to Mum in a bit more detail. But as usual, she's trying to make excuses for you. So I'm going to pack my stuff up and get out of your hair." High on adrenaline, Alex spat the words out.

"Are these the friends you're staying with?" his father asked, looking from Cam to Wicksy.

"Yes we are," Cam said, his voice rough and deeper than usual as he stepped forward, arms folded in a way that showed off the thickness of his biceps. "I suggest you stay out of our way, Mr Elliot. Alex doesn't want any more trouble, which is a shame really as I wouldn't mind giving you a taste of your own medicine."

"Me neither," Wicksy agreed. "But at least I get to tell you what a shitty excuse for a human I think you are, you disgusting, homophobic wankstain."

Alex bit back a smile as his father's face turned purple with rage.

"How dare you come here and threaten me on my own property. I should call the police." His voice rose in fury.

"Martin!" Alex's mum said in warning, taking hold of his arm.

"Great idea." Cam's voice was as smooth as syrup. "Go

for it. Phone the police, and then when they turn up Alex can explain what you did to his face."

His father knew when he was beaten. He backed away, still obviously furious, but powerless to act on his anger. "Just hurry up with whatever you need to do, and then get out of my house," he snapped.

"Gladly. Come on, guys." Alex led the way upstairs with Cam and Wicksy on his heels.

HALF AN HOUR LATER, Alex had everything he needed packed into a suitcase, a couple of smaller bags, and a carrier bag.

"You sure you don't want to bring anything else?" Cam asked, looking around at Alex's bedroom. There were still lots of things left behind: books he no longer needed, his old desktop computer that he used for gaming. Rejected items of clothing spilled out of drawers where he'd packed in a hurry. Plus he'd left behind some throwbacks to his childhood years: elaborate Lego models on a shelf, a papier-mâché T-Rex he'd made in primary school, *Star Wars* figures he used to collect.

"I've got my laptop, phone charger, the books and files I need for studying, and all the clothes I ever wear. The rest can stay." Some of the older stuff Alex would have liked for sentimental reasons, but Cam and Wicksy had so little space. He couldn't fill their living room with his crap.

"What about this guy?" Wicksy asked, picking up an old teddy bear—Bentley, Alex has christened him when he was six years old—who sat on an armchair in the corner.

Alex flushed. "I think I've outgrown teddies now."

Bentley's glass eyes seemed to stare at him reproachfully for his betrayal.

"Nah. He's cute. You can't leave him here." Wicksy tucked Bentley under his arm. "And Cam doesn't have any teddies. Buttons—my old bear from when I was a kid—needs a buddy. We can introduce them when we get back to our place."

"Seriously?" Alex wasn't sure if Wicksy was taking the piss.

"He's not joking." Cam chuckled, shaking his head. "You're a nutter, Wicksy. You'll have them going on a bloody teddy bears' picnic next. Right. Come on. Let's get out of here. I don't know about you guys but I could use a beer when we get home."

Our place. Home. Their easy acceptance of Alex into their space made Alex's chest swell with warmth. "Yeah, beer sounds good," he said. "And they're on me. Can we stop at the off-licence on the way back?"

"Sure thing." Wicksy picked up Alex's case.

"You sure you've got everything?" Cam asked, a small rucksack on his shoulder, and the carrier bag in his hand.

Alex took one last look around the room he'd slept in for as long as he could remember. What had once felt like a safe haven now felt like a prison he was escaping from.

"Yes. I'm good. Let's go."

Wicksy made a racket, deliberately bumping Alex's heavy suitcase down the polished-wood stairs, but neither of his parents emerged to protest—or to say goodbye—as they walked through the hallway. They opened the front door and Wicksy heaved the case over the threshold before wheeling it towards his car.

Alex paused on the outside of the open door and looked back. The sound of the television filtered out through the living room door, which stood ajar. He gripped his keys so tightly that they dug into his palm, and then he opened his hand.

"I don't need these anymore," he said to Cam.

Cam didn't reply, but his eyes were soft as he watched Alex, giving him time.

Alex threw the keys hard, so they landed on the tiled floor of the hall with a loud metallic sound. Then he slammed the front door, feeling nothing but relief when he was locked out on the other side of it.

"You ready to go now?" Cam asked.

Emotion had jammed Alex's throat, a lump making it impossible for him to speak. So he nodded.

Putting his free arm around Alex, Cam led him to the car.

Alex didn't look back as they drove away.

ELEVEN

Cam was glad it was a Friday night, because he felt the need for a few beers to unwind after facing Martin Elliot. Wicksy and Alex seemed to feel the same because they started drinking as soon as they got home and the drinks were going down fast. Wicksy put the TV on and found a sports channel showing MMA. "Is it bad that I wish I could do that to your dad?" he asked Alex, as a guy on the screen punched another bloke in the head.

Alex shrugged. "Not really. He deserves it."

Cam agreed entirely, but he didn't know if it was right to slag Alex's dad off all the time, no matter how much of a bastard he was. "Can we watch something else?" He had enough residual anger to deal with. Watching guys beating the crap out of each other on TV probably wasn't going to help him calm down.

"Yeah, sure." Wicksy threw the remote and Cam deftly caught it.

"What do you fancy?" he asked Alex.

"I don't really care. I'm a bit pissed already so not sure I'll be paying much attention."

"How about I put some music on instead?"

"Yeah, that's fine." Alex replied.

"Can I put the MMA on with the sound down then?" Wicksy asked.

"Sure." Cam could always ignore it. He tossed the remote back to Wicksy, and then plugged his phone into the speaker, picked a fairly upbeat Spotify playlist, and put it on shuffle.

"I should probably sort out my stuff before I drink too much more." Alex's suitcase was standing in the middle of the floor with his other bags next to it. "Where's the best place for me to keep things? I can just leave them in my case I guess." Alex looked around.

It was a small living room, and with the sofa, the armchair, the coffee table, and the TV stand taking up most of the floor space, there wasn't much room left for Alex's case. They could probably pull the sofa away from the wall for him to store it behind, but that would be a pain in the arse to have to keep getting it in and out.

"You can keep some of it in my room if you want," Cam offered. "I can free up a drawer, and I've got some plastic storage boxes in my wardrobe that I can probably empty for you. Want to come up and have a look?"

"Yeah. That would be less clutter for you and Wicksy to deal with in here, if you're sure it's not inconvenient?"

"No, it's fine. Come on." As Cam led Alex upstairs, he realised that Alex had never been in his bedroom before last night, and then only briefly. Despite all the time they'd spent together here, they'd always hung out in the living room. It hadn't been a conscious choice on Cam's part, but as he held the door open for Alex and let him inside, he felt a shift in the atmosphere between them. A frisson of tension had his skin tingling, and the memories of the kisses they'd shared back in the summer were at the forefront of his mind, unbidden.

Cam opened the door and stood aside to let Alex enter first. Alex hesitated in the doorway, staring at Cam's bed, which took up most of the room. It was a king size—ridiculous really in the relatively small bedroom—but Cam was a big guy and he loved to have enough space to sprawl. Even on the rare occasions that he'd shared his bed with someone else there was still room to spread out and get comfortable. Aside from the bed, there was just a small wardrobe, a chest of drawers, and a bedside cabinet.

"Are you sure you've got room in here for my stuff?"

Standing this close, it would have been so easy for Cam to reach out and touch him. Cam clenched his fists, digging his nails into the palms. "I can make space. Look." He eased his way past Alex and opened his wardrobe to show two storage boxes in the bottom of the hanging space. "Most of the stuff in these boxes can go to the charity shop. It's old clothes I never wear, and DVDs I haven't watched in years. I just haven't had a clear out in a while. Why don't we go down and get your things, and we can sort it out."

"Okay, thanks." Alex smiled.

Cam helped Alex carry his case and bags up. They brought more beer with them, and Cam's phone so they could listen to music up here instead, leaving Wicksy to his MMA with the sound back on.

Alex put his suitcase up on the bed and opened it, sorting his things into piles while Cam got busy making space for him.

It didn't take Cam long to bag up some things he'd be happy to see the back of—clothes he'd grown out of since his shoulders had bulked up even more with rugby training, and some old DVDs and books. That done, he managed to move some clothes he rarely wore into one of the boxes, leaving a drawer and the other box free for Alex.

"Here you go." He waved his hand at the open drawer and the empty box. "Welcome to your new home."

"Thanks." Alex grinned and raised his beer bottle where he was sitting on the edge of Cam's bed. "Here's to a new start."

Cam walked over and clinked their bottles together. "Yeah. I'll drink to that." He smiled down at Alex and their gazes locked and held.

Alex was the first to look away. "Okay, I'll get unpacked." He stood and Cam backed off to give him space.

While Alex sorted out his things, Cam sprawled on the bed and watched, drinking his beer. Having Alex putting his clothes in Cam's drawer, and in his wardrobe, gave Cam a weird sense of satisfaction, a warm rush of possessiveness that he didn't bother to question. Instead he drained his bottle—his third of the evening—and got up to fetch more. "Need another drink?"

Alex picked up his drink, which was only half-empty. "Fuck it. Yeah. Go on then." He took a few swallows. "I'm gonna feel like crap in the morning though. I should probably eat something soon."

That reminded Cam he hadn't eaten in hours either, and his stomach growled at the thought. "Yeah, me too. One more beer then we'll sort some dinner out."

"I'm nearly done here, so I'll see you downstairs in a few," Alex said.

"Okay." Cam left Alex in his room, and the weird part was that it didn't feel weird at all.

AFTER ONE MORE BEER EACH, none of them could be

bothered to attempt cooking. There were ingredients, but nothing easy they could shove in the oven.

"Let's go out and get chips," Wicksy suggested, his eyes still glued to the TV. He was sprawled on the sofa. Cam was sitting by his feet and Alex had taken the armchair. "But not till this fight is over. It's fucking awesome."

The two guys fighting were down on the mat. One had the other in a wrestling hold and their bodies writhed, slick with sweat, as the pinned guy fought to break free. "Damn this is homoerotic," Cam said, feeling a stirring in his underwear. "Why don't I watch this more often?"

"Ruin it for me why don't you?" Wicksy said. "It's not gay. It's brutal, skilful, and generally awesome. Alex, back me up here."

"I don't know." Alex was studying the screen now too. "It might be all those things, but I'm with Cam. It's also fucking hot."

That got Cam's attention off the TV and onto Alex, whose cheeks were flushed—maybe from more than the alcohol. "High five." Cam reached across the space between the sofa and armchair, hand outstretched. Alex turned and grinned, slapping his hand on Cam's.

They held each other's gazes, once again just a few beats longer than normal. Cam's heart did a weird skippy thing, and this time he was the one to break eye contact.

The fight didn't last much longer. One of the guys got knocked out in the next round. Cam felt bad for him, but it was good news for his stomach because he was ravenous. "Right, let's go and get food." He stood up too quickly, wobbling after four beers on an empty stomach. "Oops. Yeah. Definitely need to soak up some of this alcohol."

They walked down the hill into town to get fish and chips. The smell in the chippy was divine as they entered.

"I can't wait to walk home to eat them. Do you want to find a bench and eat them before we walk back up?" Cam asked once they'd been.

"Yeah, sounds good. I'm ravenous," Alex said.

"I'm gonna walk back. I want to eat mine in the warm." Wicksy shivered in his thin T-shirt.

"You should have brought a coat, you twat. It's nearly October after all," Cam said.

"Sorry, Mum."

Cam punched him on the arm. "See you back at home then."

Wicksy hurried away, while Cam and Alex walked to the harbourside and sat on a bench. They unwrapped their trays of fish and chips and dug in with fingers and plastic forks. When they were done, Alex got up to stuff their rubbish in a nearby bin, and came back to sit beside Cam. He sat close, shoulders touching. Without thinking about it, Cam put his arm along the back of the bench behind Alex.

"This is where we kissed," Alex said quietly.

Cam stiffened, his heart rate kicking up a notch. Totally focused on the need to eat, Cam hadn't realised the significance of their location. But they had ended up choosing the exact same bench where they'd sat on the night that Rainbow Place opened, when Alex had kissed Cam for the first time, and Cam had kissed him back.

Staring out at the water, Cam searched for the right thing to say to defuse this situation. But with Alex pressed up close against him and his brain foggy from beer, he couldn't think clearly. Alex turned towards him, and Cam felt warm breath on his cheek and the weight of Alex's hand on his thigh. "I still think about it, you know," Alex whispered. "I still have feelings for you. I probably shouldn't tell you that, but fuck. I don't think I'm very good at hiding it."

He moved his hand a little higher, sending arousal zinging through Cam's system.

Cam kept his gaze out on the harbour, the dark water glinting as it moved in the breeze. His heart beat wildly as desire warred with rational thought. "I... don't know what to say."

"Tell me you're not interested and I'll drop it."

"It's not that I'm not interested," Cam admitted. "I was always attracted to you. That hasn't changed. But I still think we're better as friends."

"Why?" Alex huffed, irritated. "I'm not in the closet anymore. The worst has already happened. I fucked up my exams and my dad found out about me. All your reasons for not getting involved before no longer apply." He pulled away, taking his hand off Cam's thigh, and moving out from under his arm.

Cam shifted away too, folding his arms against the chill. "But you're living in my house and our friendship is so important to me, I don't want to jeopardise it. Fuck, Alex. This isn't easy for me either you know. I'm trying to do the right thing here."

He remembered the pain of losing Leanne. Of all his friends at school, she'd been the one he always went to when he'd needed to talk. They'd shared a closeness and a connection that he hadn't truly valued until it was gone. Young and horny, he'd been all too happy to experiment with her, but hadn't wanted it to get serious. Leanne's expectations had been very different, and when Cam had realised that it was already too late to fix. Hurt, she'd withdrawn from him totally, refusing to try to salvage their friendship from the wreckage. The thought of that happening with Alex was too horrible to contemplate.

"For God's sake, Cam. Why do you have to be so serious

about everything? It's not like I want to fucking marry you or anything. I fancy you. You say you fancy me. Can't we just have some fun together as well as being friends? No strings attached, we can still see other people."

On some levels the idea was massively appealing. Cam could stop fighting his attraction and give into it. Alex seemed to know what he wanted. And he was right that the worst had already happened, how much harm could it do if they started fooling around? Just because he'd fucked up with Leanne, it didn't mean things would have to go the same way with Alex. As long as the boundaries were clear this time, then maybe he and Alex *could* still be friends afterwards, whatever happened.

No strings attached. The words echoed in Cam's brain and he baulked at them. That part also didn't sit well with him. He remembered how jealous he'd felt when Alex had told him about Ben. Cam didn't think he could handle anything casual with Alex, there was already a strong emotional connection, and fuckbuddies wouldn't be enough. If Cam was going to have Alex, he wanted him *with* strings. He wanted commitment, monogamy, and something with the potential to last.

Wow. Okay, Cam hadn't seen that coming. Maybe he was an idiot not to have realised it before, but sitting on that bench staring out at the water, he had to admit to himself that his life had slowly aligned itself so that Alex was at the centre without him even noticing.

Alex was young and inexperienced, though. He'd barely got started on life. There was no way he'd be ready to settle down in a serious relationship, not the way Cam wanted. Now he was out of the closet and out from under his parents' roof, Alex had the whole world to explore, and Cam was only one tiny part of it.

"I don't think so," he finally said. "I don't want to make things complicated. Sorry, but I value our friendship too much to risk it."

"Whatever." Alex stood. "I'm sorry I suggested it. I hope I haven't made things weird between us again."

"No. It's fine." It wasn't fine. But Cam would try and forget what Alex had suggested. He didn't want to be tempted to give in and agree to it. He stood too. "Let's go home."

They walked back in silence.

At the house, Wicksy had the TV on again, so thankfully there was no need to make conversation. Alex was on his phone, scrolling and typing, and Cam tried not to think about who he might be messaging. Feeling unsettled and wanting his own space, Cam claimed tiredness, and said he was going to bed.

"Night, guys," he said as he got up.

"Night, mate." Wicksy didn't bother to look away from the television.

"Night." Alex glanced up from his phone, his expression pinched and uncomfortable.

Cam tried to give him a reassuring smile, but he wasn't sure he pulled it off. "Hope you sleep okay once Wicksy leaves you in peace."

"Oh fuck yes, sorry, Alex. When you want to sleep just let me know, okay?" Wicksy said. "I keep forgetting I'm sitting on what's basically your bed."

"Will do," Alex replied. "I'm in no rush."

"Okay. See you in the morning." Cam left the room, pulling the door shut behind him so the television wouldn't keep him awake.

TWELVE

It took a couple of days for Alex to feel comfortable around Cam again. Fortunately, he was working at Rainbow Place both days over the weekend, so they didn't spend too much time together. He bitterly regretted the conversation with Cam on Friday night. He blamed the alcohol for his poor decision and wished he could turn the clock back. After their all-too-brief fling in the summer—could you even call two lots of kissing and a one-sided hand job a fling?—they'd managed to forge a friendship that Alex treasured. He'd been stupid to put that in jeopardy again. If Alex was being honest with himself he knew that no-strings fun with Cam would only lead to heartbreak. Alex's feelings for Cam ran way deeper than attraction alone and he didn't think he'd be able to keep them separate.

Thankfully, Wicksy was around on both Saturday and Sunday night. His presence was a buffer, his banter and lighthearted humour giving some much-needed light relief when things were tense between Alex and Cam. Alex wondered how much Wicksy knew, and how much he noticed. He put on a good act of being oblivious, but Alex suspected he picked up on more than he let on.

Having his things in Cam's room wasn't ideal given the tension between them. On Sunday night, Alex showered before bed, and forgot to take clean clothes to change into afterwards. Leaving his dirty underwear and T-shirt in the laundry basket, he wrapped a towel around his waist and picked up his sweatpants before going to tap on Cam's door.

"Come in."

Cam was lying on his bed dressed only in boxer briefs and a threadbare grey T-shirt. Neither left much to the imagination, the fabric clinging to the curves, planes, and bulges of Cam's impressive body. He had his phone in one hand and looked up as Alex came in.

"Hey, sorry. I forgot to get clean clothes out," Alex said, clutching his towel. He felt his cheeks heat as he tried not to stare.

Alex felt exposed as Cam's gaze raked over him. Wishing he'd put his dirty T-shirt back on to cover his pale, skinny body, he hurried over to the chest of drawers and bent to open his drawer and get out some new boxers and a T-shirt. As he rummaged around, he dropped his sweatpants, and bent lower to pick them up. His towel slipped and he felt cool air on his arse as it was exposed. *Fuck.* He quickly grabbed his towel, yanking it back up before it fell off completely.

Turning, cheeks flaming, he caught Cam's eyes on him before he snapped his gaze back to his phone.

He'd definitely been looking at Alex's arse, and had got to see rather more of it than he'd been expecting. Alex's mind scrabbled desperately for something funny to say to break the awkward silence.

Enjoying the show?

Didn't you know it was a full moon tonight?

But all he could think about was Cam staring at his butt, and how much Alex wanted him to do more than look. The thought of that made his dick start to take notice. He'd already embarrassed himself enough for tonight, so Alex went back to his rummaging, grabbed the first clothes he could find, and made a swift exit, clutching his clothes in front of his semi.

"Cheers. Night," he muttered as he went.

"Night," Cam replied quietly.

LIVING with someone you had a king-sized crush on should be a form of torture, Alex decided. He hadn't realised how different it would feel staying under the same roof as Cam. Seeing him in his sleep clothes, or meeting him on the landing wearing nothing but a towel, going into his room in the morning and seeing his rumpled bedclothes— probably still warm and smelling of him. These things conspired to make Alex feel a little crazy with want. He began to wonder whether he'd made a mistake in choosing to stay here rather than taking Seb up on his offer of a room. No longer trusting his own judgement, he decided he needed some perspective, so he called Hayden on his way down to Rainbow Place on Friday morning.

Hayden answered after a few rings. "Ugh. What's up?" His voice was rough with sleep.

"Oh sorry. I didn't mean to wake you. I thought you had college this morning and I'd catch you on the bus."

Hayden's bed creaked. "Fuck! What time is it? Oh shit. I've gotta go."

"Hang on! I need to talk to you, are you around later?"

"What day is it?"

"Friday."

"Yeah. I finish at lunchtime today. Wanna meet for coffee?"

"I'm working till four; can you meet me at Rainbow Place then?"

"Sure." Frantic rustling indicated Hayden was up and getting dressed.

"Okay," Alex said. "See you later."

"Yeah. Bye."

ALEX WAS STARTING to really enjoy working at Rainbow Place. The first couple of days had been a bit stressful while he was learning new skills and getting used to everything. Plus it had been really busy during both his weekend shifts. During the week that had passed since then, he'd managed to get to grips with things when it was a little more sedate and he wasn't running around quite as frantically.

He and Dylan were serving and taking orders today, while Tom helped Luca in the kitchen. Seb was mostly based in the kitchen today too, because he was discussing some new menu ideas with Luca as they worked.

"It's interesting who we get in here." Leaning against the bar during the mid-morning lull, Dylan let his gaze roam over the tables, taking in the range of customers. From toddlers with their mums, to a group of elderly ladies who Alex already recognised as regulars. "Such a mixture. It's cool." He focused on a man sitting in the far corner by the window. "That guy is sexy. Have you seen him in here before?"

Following Dylan's laser-intense gaze, Alex studied the guy

who was dressed in jeans and a navy fisherman's jumper. Busy doing something on his laptop with a notebook on the table beside him, the man was oblivious to their scrutiny. "Yeah," Alex said. "I'm pretty sure he was here at least one other morning this week. You think he's hot?" With his jumper, mid-length dark hair that was messy and greying at the temples, and silver-framed glasses, he reminded Alex of his old Geography teacher. Definitely not Alex's type, although he supposed that objectively he was quite handsome.

"He's gorgeous. Older geeky guys are like crack to me." Straightening up, Dylan ran a hand through his red curls. "Do you reckon he's gay?"

"Hard to tell. He isn't wearing a T-shirt that says *Giant Homo* on it, so how on earth would we know?" Alex said dryly.

"I'm going to see if he wants more coffee," Dylan said. He fussed with his hair again, and then grinned at Alex. "Wish me luck."

"Good luck."

Alex watched as Dylan walked confidently over to the man's table. He couldn't have listened in from this distance and gave up watching when one of the mums of the toddlers came up to order more tea and a couple of pieces of flapjack.

By the time Alex had dealt with her, Dylan was back, busy with the coffee machine.

"How did it go?" Alex asked.

"Not exactly stellar," Dylan admitted. "He did want coffee, and I think he might be gay because there was something about the way he looked at me... but he's terminally shy and awkward so I couldn't get much of a conversation going." He sighed. "He's even hotter close-up too. He had really nice hands, and hairy wrists. I bet he has loads of chest hair under that jumper."

Alex chuckled. "Well keep working on it. If he's a regular you should get plenty of chances."

"True." Dylan brightened at the prospect. "Maybe he'll warm up eventually. Okay, I'll take this over to him."

HAYDEN SHOWED up ten minutes before Alex was due to finish.

"Hey, dude. How's it going?" Hayden leant over the bar and hooked a hand around the back of Alex's neck, pulling him in for a kiss on the cheek.

Alex flushed at the display of affection, and then reminded himself that here—of all places—nobody would think it was inappropriate. "I'm not bad thanks. It's really good to see you."

"Yeah. I'm sorry I didn't manage to catch up with you sooner." Hayden's gaze lit on Alex's cheek where the bruises had almost faded, but the cut had left a pink scar. "I still can't believe your dad hit you. What a complete cunt."

"Shh!" Alex glanced around in alarm, hoping no customers had overheard Hayden and been offended by his choice of words. "But yeah. He really is."

"So how is it working out staying with Cam?" Hayden grinned and waggled his eyebrows. "Any action yet?"

"No," Alex said, and Hayden's grin faded. "Can we talk when I've finished my shift? I won't be long. Do you want a coffee while you wait?"

"Sure. Can I get mates' rates?"

"It's on me. I can use my staff discount anyway. Latte?"

"Please."

"Go and grab a table where we can chat and I'll bring it over."

HAYDEN WAS HALFWAY DOWN his large latte when Alex joined him with a coffee for himself. Sitting opposite Hayden, Alex sighed. "God it's good to sit down. I'm knackered."

"Long day?"

"The usual. I'm always tired when I finish after being on my feet all day."

"How's it going working here?"

"I love it." Alex smiled. "Seb's a great boss. And all the other people who work here are nice."

"Are most of them queer?"

Alex shrugged. "Hard to know unless they tell me. Dylan definitely is. I think Tom might be, but he hasn't said. I'm not sure about anyone else." He took a sip of his coffee. "So how's college going?"

"It awesome." Hayden's face lit up. "I've met so many new people and I'm having a brilliant time. Trouble is all the partying is costing me a fortune. I need to rein it in a bit."

Alex felt a flash of envy. He should have been off at uni making new friends and having fun. But he was making new friends through his job, and at least he wasn't stuck doing Business Studies. "That's cool. And is the course okay?"

"Yeah, it's pretty good. I'm definitely learning a lot." He examined Alex's hair critically. "You could do with a haircut actually. Will you let me practise on you?"

"Maybe."

"So, anyway. You were going to tell me about your new

living arrangements. How's that going? And is it a perma-
nent thing?"

"No. It can only be for a while. Cam and Wicksy don't
have a spare room so I'm sleeping on the sofa. They've been
awesome about it, but it can't be convenient for them having
me taking up their living room. I should probably start
trying to sort out something else; maybe rent a place once
I've saved up for a deposit."

"And there's still nothing going on with you and Cam?"
Hayden looked so disappointed it would have been amusing
if Alex hadn't felt exactly the same.

"No." Alex lowered his voice. "And it's been really
awkward this week because I basically propositioned him
last Friday when I was drunk, and he turned me down—
again. So that was fun."

"Ouch." Hayden made a sympathetic face. "I don't get
it, though. It's always been obvious that he fancies you.
Why the fuck won't he do something about it now you've
made the break from your parents?"

"I don't know. He says it's because he doesn't want to
spoil our friendship, but I'm not sure. Maybe he's gone off
me and doesn't think of me that way anymore. Whatever
the reasons, it makes living there difficult because ugh.
Hayden, I fancy him so much, and he's such a great guy,
and it's like *torture* being around him all the time but not
being able to have what I really want." As the words
tumbled out, Alex's emotions flooded with them like a dam
bursting. He hadn't realised how much he'd been keeping a
lid on until now. His heart ached and his eyes burnt with
tears that he blinked away. "It's too hard."

"Shit, man. I'm sorry." Hayden reached across and put a
hand on Alex's arm. "That does sound tough." The fact that

Hayden avoided making the obvious *hard* joke showed how seriously he was taking Alex's plight.

"I do have another option, and I'm wondering if I should take it." Alex glanced over at Seb who was standing near the bar. His boyfriend, Jason, had just arrived, still in his dusty work clothes and heavy boots. As Alex watched, they exchanged a lingering kiss. Seb's smile was radiant as he drew away, saying something Alex couldn't hear. "Seb said I can have his spare room for as long as I need. He made the offer the day I left home, but I wanted to be with Cam. Now I think maybe I made a stupid decision and should see if Seb's offer still stands."

"Yeah. It would probably be the sensible option. You'd have a room to yourself, and a bit of space between you and Cam sounds like a good thing if it's messing you up living in such close proximity."

"Mmm." Alex knew Hayden was right. But he didn't want to be sensible. He wanted Cam to change his mind. "I'll think about it over the weekend."

"Speaking of the weekend, it's Friday night. I'm going into St Austell to meet some people from college. You wanna come with me? There are lots of cute gay guys on my course. You'd have no trouble pulling if you want someone to take your mind off Cam."

"I already tried finding someone to take my mind off Cam, and look how well that turned out." Alex rolled his eyes. "My dad caught us, and I'm more obsessed with Cam than ever."

"Yeah, well your dad won't be around to spoil your fun this time. Go on. Come out with me. It'll be awesome. My mate Ashley said I can crash at his place. He won't mind me bringing you along."

Alex considered it for a moment, but no. "Thanks, man, but not this evening. I'm knackered and not really in the mood to party." He'd stayed up late the night before finishing and submitting a Sociology essay, and he had to be at work for the early shift on Saturday. If Hayden had been going out in Porthladock he might have joined him, as he could have walked home if he wasn't feeling it. He didn't fancy being stuck in St Austell for the night with no way of getting home. If he decided he wanted to be sociable later, there was some fundraiser thing at the rugby club tonight that Wicksy had mentioned.

"Okay. Maybe another time then?"

"Yeah."

Hayden checked the time on his phone. "Right, I'd better shoot off. Need to get home and eat before I go out again." He stood, and Alex got up too. They hugged each other and Hayden gave Alex an extra squeeze. "I'm sorry you've been having a shitty time of it. Call me whenever you need, okay? I hope things get better soon."

"Thanks, Hayden."

"Cam's an idiot by the way. And it's totally his loss. You're awesome."

Alex grinned, spirits lifting a little. "Cheers. Glad you think so."

THIRTEEN

"You coming down the rugby club tonight?" Wicksy asked Cam as they rubbed shoulders in the cramped kitchen. Wicksy was making bacon, egg, and beans, while Cam was cooking pasta. Luckily Alex had eaten earlier and was currently upstairs showering.

"I dunno. Maybe."

There was a seventies tribute band playing there tonight as a fundraiser for the club. Cam knew he ought to put in an appearance to support it, but after a long week clearing a massively overgrown garden, he was more in the mood for lounging on the sofa at home with a beer.

"I reckon it will be a right laugh. Loads of people are going, and the band's supposed to be good. I asked Alex this morning and he said he might come."

That piqued Cam's interest. If he was honest with himself part of his motivation for staying in was the hope that he could hang out with Alex. Things had been a bit off between them this week—unsurprisingly—and he'd been hoping they could get past that and have a nice evening together. But if Alex was going out, Cam didn't fancy staying in on his own. "Yeah. I'll probably come out for a bit then."

THEY GOT down to the club just after eight to find it was already busy. The band hadn't started yet but speakers were pumping out seventies disco music.

"You didn't tell me it was fancy dress!" Alex said, looking around.

"It's only optional," Wicksy replied. "Wow, look at that woman in the silver all-in-one thing. She looks hot as fuck."

Cam followed his gaze to see a brunette in a shiny silver cat suit and high platform boots. She had a rocking body and did indeed look amazing in the outfit. "Yeah. She looks great," he agreed.

"When you two have finished drooling, do either of you want a drink?" Alex asked. There was an edge to his voice that caught Cam's attention.

As he turned back, Cam replied, "Yeah. A pint of lager please. I'll come and help you carry them."

"Same," said Wicksy, still staring at the woman. "I think I'm in love. Who the hell is she? I've never seen her round here before. I wonder if she's single."

Alex and Cam made their way to the bar. They had to wait a while to get served and when they emerged, drinks in hand, Cam looked around to see where Wicksy had got to.

"Surprise, surprise." He jerked his head towards where Wicksy was chatting to the brunette over at the side of the room. She smiled, and then laughed at something Wicksy said. "Looks like it's going well."

As they approached, the woman saw them coming before Wicksy did. Her eyes flitted over Alex and settled on Cam, raking up his torso before meeting his eyes and holding his gaze. She smiled, and that's when Wicksy turned to see them.

"Oh, hey, guys. Thanks for the beer. Alex, Cam, this is Viola. She's Luca's cousin—visiting from Italy."

Viola offered them a slim, perfectly manicured hand to shake. Alex first and then Cam. Her hand lingered in his for a moment. Enchanted by her deep brown eyes and the curve of her full lips, Cam smiled.

Alex cleared his throat and Cam released Viola's hand as Alex asked, "So, Viola. Are you staying long or is it a short trip?" Something in his tone made it sound as if he was hoping for the latter.

"For a couple of weeks only, I'm afraid. Just a holiday before I go back to Italy to start a new job." The words were fluent but her accent was strong.

There was an awkward silence.

"Are you enjoying it so far?" Cam could still feel the tension rippling off Alex beside him.

"Yes," she said effusively. "It's very beautiful here. The sea, the coastline. I live inland so this is magical for me."

"What sightseeing have you got planned?" Wicksy asked, sidling a little closer to her. He shot Cam a quick glance that said, *Please fuck off. I saw her first.*

A few months ago, Cam might have stayed to talk. He and Wicksy often liked the same women when they went out on the pull and sometimes engaged in a little friendly rivalry while trying to woo the same girl. Both of them were pretty good-natured about it if one succeeded where the other failed, and if both of them got turned down they'd drown their sorrows together instead.

Tonight Cam was happy to back off and let Wicksy chat her up alone. Alex was obviously jealous, and Cam didn't want to upset him by flirting with Viola when he had no intention of doing anything even if she was interested. She was stunning, but Cam was too wrapped up in his complicated feelings for Alex to be distracted by her.

He put his hand on Alex's arm. "Hey, look. There's Seb and Jason. Shall we go and say hello?"

"Okay." Alex relaxed and gave Cam a small smile.

"Excuse us," Cam said to Viola. "It was nice to meet you. Have fun in Cornwall."

"Thank you." Her smile held a hint of regret, but then she turned back to Wicksy. "So, what local sights should I make sure I see?"

Alex stuck close to Cam's side as they crossed the room. "She was really into you," he said. "I think Wicksy's out of luck."

Cam shrugged. "Well so is she. I'm not interested."

"Really?" Alex's sidelong glance was sceptical.

"She's beautiful but I'm not looking for a holiday fling."

"What are you looking for?"

Cam stopped in his tracks and Alex turned to look at him. It was a good question. What the hell did he want? A few months ago he'd have been happy with his life. Young, free, and single, enjoying the occasional hook-up and some very casual dating. It had suited him just fine. Now he was celibate and fighting feelings for someone who had become his new best friend. He felt disloyal to Wicksy for thinking that, but it was true. Wicksy was a top bloke and Cam loved him dearly, but Alex was different. With Alex there was that emotional connection that he'd had with Leanne. Their connection ran deep and Cam couldn't imagine his life without Alex in it.

"I have no idea," he finally answered with a shrug. The answer to that question would have to wait. It was Friday night, he had a beer in his hand, and he wanted to chill.

"You coming?" He jerked his head towards where Seb and Jason were sitting at a table at the edge of the room.

"Sure."

"Hey, guys, is anyone sitting here, or can we join you?" Cam asked when they reached the table.

"Hi, and no. Feel free."

They greeted each other with handshakes and smiles. Jason and Seb were sitting side by side on a bench seat, so Cam and Alex took the chairs opposite them. As they sat down, Seb moved closer to Jason, and Jason put his arm around him.

"So how are things going with you, Alex?" Jason asked. "You enjoying working at Rainbow Place? Seb isn't being too much of a slave driver I hope."

"Oi!" Seb said.

Jason grinned and gave him a quick kiss on the cheek.

"No." Alex chuckled. "It's cool. I enjoy it. It's way better than working on the caravan site out of season even though it's pretty hectic. I'd rather be busy than bored."

They sat and talked for a while as the club filled up even more around them. When Cam's glass was empty, he stood. "It's my round, are you ready for another?" he asked Alex.

"Yes please."

"Can I get you guys a drink too?"

"Oh, are you sure? We can just get our own," Seb said.

"No, no. It's fine. Let me get these. What do you want?"

"A pint of lager for me—Stella please," Jason said.

"And I'll have vodka and Diet Coke. Thank you." Seb swirled the ice in the bottom of his almost-empty glass.

"Want me to help carry?" Alex offered.

"Yes please."

As they crossed the room they encountered a vision in

white flared trousers and a garishly patterned shirt open to the waist to reveal a broad hairy chest, and a gold medallion. He was clutching a half-empty pint in one hand.

"Hey, Cam, Alex! Great to see you." As he was also wearing a wig, it took Cam a moment to recognise Drew, his team captain. He looked to be a few beers down from his loose posture and booming voice.

"Jesus, Drew. That's quite a costume." Cam let Drew pull him into a backslapping hug, and then pulled back to examine his costume more closely. "You look ridiculous."

"That's exactly the look I was going for." Drew grinned, turned to Alex, and hugged him too. "It's great to see you both." His expression darkened. "I heard about what happened with your father, mate. If there's anything me or any of the lads can do, you only have to ask."

"Thanks," Alex said. "I appreciate that. But every-thing's okay now I don't have to live there anymore. My dad is basically acting as though I don't exist and that's fine by me." He tried to sound cheerful but Cam could detect bitterness lacing Alex's words.

"Anyway, it's great to see you together. About bloody time as far as I can tell. You've been dancing around each other ever since you first met."

It took a moment for the meaning of his words to sink in. Alex had worked it out before Cam did. "Oh no," he said quickly. "We're not together like that. We're just friends." He glanced at Cam, looking uncomfortable.

"But I heard you'd moved in together?"

"Yeah, but not as a couple. I'm sleeping on their sofa for a while."

"Oh, sorry. My bad." Drew grinned at them, seemingly unabashed by his faux-pas. "Well I'd have put money on you two getting together, so why the hell hasn't it happened yet? No, don't worry. You don't have to answer that." He patted Cam on the shoulder. "Right, I'm going to go and check on the band and see if they're ready to start soon. See you boys later. Have fun." With that he squeezed past them through the throng of people and was gone.

"Well that was fucking awkward," Alex said.

"Yeah." Drew's words still rang in Cam's ears: *Why the hell hasn't it happened yet?* He was starting to wonder the same thing. Why was he fighting so hard against something that was beginning to feel inevitable?

"Come on." Alex tugging on his arm brought Cam's attention back. "Let's get to the bar before there's an even bigger queue."

"THAT WAS A REALLY WICKED NIGHT," Wicksy said, his speech slurred from alcohol. "I don't even like Abba, but that band was awesome. I think I pulled something dancing though. Maybe a groin strain."

Alex laughed, and Cam snorted. "You'd better not have. We need you to be fit for our match against Newquay next weekend."

"Would have been an even better night if I'd pulled though," Wicksy carried on as though Cam hadn't spoken. "That Viola, she was so fucking gorgeous." He sighed loudly. "But she wasn't interested. She only wanted to dance with me, nothing else."

"You can't win 'em all." Cam patted him on the back, and then grabbed his arm as he stumbled. They were all a little drunk—even Alex, who was working in the morning—but Wicksy was definitely the most inebriated of the three of them.

"She liked you. Asked me about you after you'd gone.

She thought you were gay. Told her you're bi, but unavailable."

"What? Why would you say that?"

"'S true innit." Wicksy shrugged. "You might be officially single but you haven't shown any interest in anyone in months. Not since—"

"Drew's costume was brilliant," Cam said. "He looked hilarious. But the best part was when he split his trousers doing a slut drop on the dance floor. Thank fuck he was wearing underwear is all I can say."

They all laughed at that.

"Yeah," Wicksy said. "I wish I'd got a costume. Next time they do something like that I'm gonna make more of an effort."

Relieved he'd managed to steer Wicksy onto a different conversational course, Cam relaxed a little. He and Wicksy discussed some of the other costumes people had worn at the party for the rest of the walk home, but Alex remained silent. Cam suspected he knew all too well what Wicksy had been about to say.

Cam hadn't shown any interest in anyone else since he'd met Alex.

Why the hell hasn't it happened yet? That question echoed in his brain again, and this time he answered: *Because you're scared.* He was afraid of fucking up, of hurting Alex, of being hurt, of ruining what they already had.

Back at the house, Wicksy headed straight for the living room while Cam went to the kitchen. He and Alex made toast and drank orange juice. They ate in the kitchen, leaning against the counter. Alex was typing on his phone and Cam watched him surreptitiously, admiring his profile, and the fullness of his lips. He tried to imagine them being in a relationship. Would it work? Should they try? Did Alex still even want that? Did he?

He sighed and shook his head as though to clear out the confused fog of his thoughts.

"You okay?" Alex asked.

"Yeah. Just tired. I'm gonna head up to bed."

They held each other's gaze for a moment and the connection was there as always. The pull that Cam was getting tired of resisting.

"Night then," Alex said, expression impossible to read.

"Night."

In his room, Cam stripped down to his boxers then went to piss and brush his teeth. When he came out of the bathroom, Alex was waiting on the landing.

"It's all yours," Cam said, gesturing to the bathroom door.

"Um. Yeah. But we have a problem. Wicksy's passed out on the sofa—like utterly dead-to-the-world asleep. I tried poking him, but short of literally tipping him off onto the floor there's no way I can shift him. Do you think he'd mind if I sleep in his room tonight?"

"I'm sure he wouldn't. But have you seen his room? Wicksy's a pig. He probably hasn't changed his sheets in months." Cam wasn't exaggerating. Wicksy was a lazy fucker and his room was usually a pit.

"It can't be that bad," Alex said, opening the door, and flicking the light on. "Oh wow. Okay. I see what you mean."

Cam looked over his shoulder. No carpet was visible through the piles of clothes on the floor. The bed was rumpled and the dark-grey sheets had some questionable-looking stains on them. As Cam inhaled he wrinkled his nose, the air was stale, and smelt of dirty laundry. "Yeah. You don't want to sleep in here." He paused, ignoring the way his heart rate kicked up a notch before casually asking, "You want to share my bed? It's plenty big enough for two."

Alex turned, his expression wary. "You sure?"

"Of course." Cam tried to make it sound like it was no big deal. And really it shouldn't have been. Two mates sharing a bed wasn't exactly unusual. He'd shared with Wicksy in hotels before for weekends away when they couldn't get twins. But sharing a bed with Alex would be a big deal, and they both knew it.

There was a long pause while Cam's heart thumped erratically. He couldn't decide if he wanted Alex to accept or refuse.

"Okay," Alex said. "I'll go and do my teeth and stuff. See you in a minute."

Heart still pounding, Cam was afraid he might actually hyperventilate before Alex joined him. He hurried around, fussing with his already-tidy room, and then pulled a T-shirt on. He normally slept just in boxers because his duvet was thick and very warm. *God*, he was overthinking things. Ripping the T-shirt off again, he stuffed it back in his drawer, and got into bed. Closing his eyes, he waited, listening to the sounds of water running and the flush of the toilet. Next came the creak of the floorboards on the landing and the soft click of Alex closing the bedroom door behind him.

"Hey," Alex said quietly.

Cam considered pretending to be asleep. Maybe that would be for the best, but as he heard the rustle of clothing he couldn't resist opening his eyes to watch Alex stepping out of his jeans. "Hey," he replied, propping himself up on his elbows. The duvet slipped off his bare shoulders and Alex's gaze dropped, taking in Cam's shirtlessness.

In a slow, deliberate movement, Alex lifted his T-shirt

over his head to reveal his fair skin and slim, toned body. When his head emerged, he held Cam's gaze as though in challenge while he tossed the T-shirt over the back of a chair. Cam lay back, holding his breath as Alex walked around and climbed into the other side of the bed. There was the dip and creak of the mattress and then Alex was lying on his back beside Cam. Stretching out an arm, Cam turned off the lamp by the bed.

The sudden darkness was as thick as velvet.

Cam wondered whether Alex was as nervous as he was. The weight of possibility filled the space between them, and Cam was powerless to resist the temptation to reach out and bridge the gap. He found Alex's hand and took it, wordlessly threading their fingers together. He squeezed, and Alex returned the pressure.

Taking a shaky breath, Cam edged closer until he could feel the heat of Alex's body alongside his. He rubbed his thumb in tiny circles on Alex's wrist and Alex squeezed his hand again.

Cam wasn't sure who made the first move. They seemed to roll onto their sides as one, reaching for each other in the darkness. It started as a hug; bodies pressed together, their faces buried in each other's shoulders. The scent of Alex's skin made Cam's gut twist with longing and his body flushed hot, dick hardening between them in a way that surely Alex had to notice.

"Cam?" Alex's voice was uncertain.

"Yeah?" Cam's voice was muffled by Alex's neck where he was breathing him in. A rapid pulse beat against his lips.

"What are we doing?"

"I don't know."

Cam turned his face, searching for Alex's mouth with his own.

When their lips finally met, all Cam's reservations were washed away by the perfect press of Alex's kiss, by the sigh Alex gave that sounded like relief. Finally, after months of holding back, Cam gave himself up to the inevitable like a ship washed away on the tide.

FOURTEEN

What are we doing?

Alex's own words played on a loop in his head, but he ignored them, and kissed Cam harder. He was afraid this would only be for one night, afraid of being hurt, but he wanted Cam too much to put a stop to this even though he knew that would be the sensible thing to do.

Instead he hooked his leg over Cam's hip and pulled their bodies even closer so he could feel the hardness of Cam's erection and press his own against it.

Cam groaned and reached down to cup Alex's arse and squeeze. The tiny amount of space between them was still too much for Alex. He clung to Cam like a limpet to a rock as though he was trying to meld them into one. Arousal flushed his skin and pooled in his groin like molten metal, the heavy drag of it wonderful and frustrating all at once.

Determined not to make an idiot of himself by coming too soon this time, Alex broke the kiss, and pushed firmly on Cam's chest. "Lie on your back," he whispered.

"What do you want?" Cam asked.

"I want to suck your cock. Is that okay?"

"Yeah," Cam's reply was breathless. "Course. Or... we could sixty-nine if you want?"

"Okay." Alex had never done that, but he wasn't going to say no to Cam's mouth on his dick. "How do you want to do it?"

"Kneel over me."

They shed their underwear and Alex positioned himself over Cam on hands and knees. "Like this?"

"Yeah, perfect." Cam's warm breath brushed his balls.

Although he wished he could see more of Cam, Alex was grateful for the darkness. With his arse over Cam's face he felt incredibly self-conscious even though Cam could barely see anything. Turning his attention to Cam, Alex guided Cam's cock into his mouth and started to suck and Cam did the same to him.

The sensory overload of hot suction on his dick and the feeling of Cam in his mouth soon had Alex flying high, all awkwardness forgotten. He moaned as Cam's fingertips stroked behind his balls and edged back towards his hole.

"This okay?" Cam pulled off to ask, one hand a vice around Alex's dick.

"Yes," Alex managed, voice a hoarse croak, before going back to sucking.

Cam's fingers were wet with spit as he rubbed them over Alex's hole and Alex moaned, pushing back against them, desperately craving more. But he was getting close now and wasn't ready to come yet. He let Cam's cock slip from his mouth again so he could gasp, "Stop!"

Cam froze. "Sorry, is that too much?"

"Not in a bad way. But I'm going to come if you carry on and I don't want to. Not yet."

"Oh." Cam's voice was warm with amusement. "That's

okay. We can slow things down a bit. What do you want to do?"

"Maybe give my dick a break, but carry on... with the other stuff." Alex's cheeks flushed hot.

"You want me to play with your arse?"

"Yes."

"Would you like me to lick it?"

Alex's cheeks burnt even hotter as his cock jerked in Cam's hand—a pretty clear yes even without him saying anything. "If you want to."

"I'd love to." Cam slapped him gently on the butt. "Move forward a little."

Alex obeyed, his dick suddenly cool as Cam let go of it to get both his hands on Alex's arse cheeks and spread him open.

"I wish I could see you," Cam said. "I bet you look fucking gorgeous like this." Imagining Cam looking at him in this position made Alex's body hot all over. "Now get back to sucking my cock while I lick your arse."

The order gave Alex a thrill. He liked that Cam was taking charge; it made him feel safe. Obediently, he parted his lips around the head of Cam's dick, and started to suck again. The wet touch of Cam's tongue on his hole made him moan, taking Cam deeper. Rimming was another thing Alex had never experienced, and now he understood why people did it. It was sweet torture, a little ticklish, a lot sensitive, and it felt so incredibly intimate. Soon Alex had lost all his inhibitions again and was rocking back and forth on Cam's face, taking his cock so deep in his throat that his eyes were streaming. Even without stimulation on his dick, he was hard and leaking, close to the edge but in no imminent danger of falling. Gradually the need for more built until he couldn't stand it any longer.

Pulling off Cam's cock, he gasped, "Will you fuck me?"

Cam squeezed Alex's arse, fingers digging in as he asked, "You sure?"

"Why wouldn't I be sure?" It was bizarre having a conversation in this position, Alex's arse over Cam's face, and Cam's dick rubbing his cheek.

"Have you done it before?"

"No." Alex huffed in frustration. "But so what? I know what I want. Stop treating me like a kid."

There was a pause, and Alex's heart sank. If Cam put a stop to this now he'd be devastated. At that point in time, Alex didn't care about the past or the future. The only thing that mattered was the present and his whole body ached for Cam. Whatever happened tomorrow morning, he knew he wouldn't regret taking this chance.

"Okay," Cam said finally. "Get off me then. I'll have to put the lamp on so I can find some lube and a condom."

Alex's stomach lurched as the reality of what he was about to do hit home. Nerves and excitement rippled through him as he climbed off Cam to lie on his back on the bed. He reached down to stroke his cock, which had softened a little during their discussion.

There was a click, and soft light flooded the room. Cam was sitting on the edge of the bed rummaging in the drawer with his broad back towards Alex, the width of his shoulders blocking the light. Alex shivered in anticipation, his cock thickening again.

When Cam turned, his smile was soft, and his eyes were full of something that made Alex's heart swell and his nerves dissipate. The sight of Cam's thick cock rearing up only made Alex long to be filled by it even though he'd never had more than one of his own fingers in him before.

He trusted Cam.

"Roll over and lie flat," Cam said. Although his voice was gentle there was that hint of command to it from before.

Lying on his front, head pillowed on his forearms, Alex felt the dip of the mattress as Cam moved behind him. He pushed Alex's legs wider and Alex let Cam move him how he wanted. Strong hands gripped his buttocks and spread him, and he was rewarded with Cam's tongue stroking over his hole again. Soon, Alex was right back at the point where he was desperately craving more.

"Please, Cam," he moaned, not sure exactly what he was asking for. He lifted his hips and rutted against the bed, his cock dragging against the sheets where it was trapped under his body.

Cam shifted, and there was the sound of rustling and the click of a bottle cap. He leant low over Alex, straddling his hips, and kissing the back of his neck before working his way down Alex's spine. "You're gorgeous," he said. Fingers, slippery with lube, rubbed over Alex's hole. Whimpering, Alex pushed back against them making Cam chuckle softly. "Gorgeous and eager. We need to take this slow if it's your first time. Just relax and let me take care of you." He kneed Alex's thighs wider as he pushed a finger inside.

Alex gasped and tensed, and then forced himself to do what Cam had told him and relaxed. As he let go, Cam's finger slipped in easily, lighting up mysterious nerve endings, and sending tingles of pleasure through Alex's body. He lost track of time as Cam fucked him slowly with that finger. After a while there was a brief, burning stretching sensation as Cam added another, making Alex tense up again before he accepted that one too. He was flying again, lost in the feeling of his cock rubbing the sheets as he rocked his hips in counterpoint to the insistent push of Cam's fingers inside him.

"You ready for my cock?" Cam asked.

"Yes." Alex was more than ready. He was primed, desperate, craving that connection beyond anything. He hissed as Cam withdrew his fingers, his body clinging to them, the slight friction giving an edge of discomfort.

"Sorry. I'll use plenty of lube for my cock. Lift up." Cam's strong hands guided Alex until he was on hands and knees. "That's perfect. God, you look so hot, Alex."

Alex looked over his shoulder to admire Cam for a moment. It seemed ludicrous that such a perfect-looking human would consider Alex hot, but Alex wasn't complaining. He let his head drop as Cam moved in close behind him. There was pressure on his hole, teasing as Cam slid the head of his cock up and down, not quite pushing hard enough to get his dick inside.

"Cam, please!" Alex's voice rose in frustration.

"Yeah. You want it?" Cam sounded hoarse, tight with desire.

"Yes." Alex pushed back against him. They both gasped as the tip pressed in. Eager for more, Alex pushed back harder, and then regretted it as a sharp spike of pain made him grunt in discomfort. "Ow, fuck!" He froze, and so did Cam.

"You okay?"

"Yes, well... not exactly. Just give me a minute," Alex managed through gritted teeth. His cock had softened; the pain a bucket of icy water to his libido.

"Breathe."

Cam smoothed warm palms over Alex's back up to his shoulders, squeezing the muscles there as Alex took a slow breath in. As he exhaled, the pain eased, replaced by stretch and pressure that was weird, but good.

"Are you all the way in?" Alex asked.

"Just about." Cam sounded amused. "You were impatient."

"Yeah, well. I've been waiting a while for this." The words escaped before Alex could stop them, but Cam didn't react.

"Do you want the rest?"

"Yep. Do it."

The final thrust of Cam's cock stole Alex's breath. There was no more pain but the fullness was intense.

Cam withdrew and pushed back in slowly a few times. "How does that feel?"

"Bizarre," Alex managed breathlessly. His cock was taking an interest again. He reached down to give it a stroke, glad to feel it hardening under his touch.

"In a good way?"

"Definitely in a good way." As Cam fucked him, gradually increasing the speed and force of his thrusts, Alex felt his body lighting up, arousal building again. With his hand on his dick and the drag of Cam's cock in his arse, Alex felt his climax approaching, and this time he didn't want to resist. "Think I'm gonna come soon."

"Thank fuck for that," Cam said breathlessly. "Cos so am I."

Alex laughed, wild elation bubbling up inside him. He stroked his cock faster as Cam ploughed into him. The bed was creaking and banging against the wall, and Alex didn't even care if Wicksy woke up and heard them. A few more strokes of his hand and thrusts of Cam's cock and he was coming, white-hot pleasure exploding as he came all over the bed in a series of mind-blowing spurts. "Oh fuck. Yes," he cried out, and Cam groaned, pushing in deep, hips jerking as he came too.

Finally, they stilled, both breathing hard. Cam was the first to speak. "You okay?"

"I'm awesome," Alex replied, in a blissful, post-coital haze.

Cam leant forward and kissed Alex's shoulder before carefully pulling out. Alex collapsed gratefully onto his front, not caring about the sticky patch, while Cam dealt with the condom. Then Cam was back beside Alex, one arm over his back as he kissed Alex's cheek, and murmured, "That was amazing."

Sleepy now, Alex rolled onto his side so he could kiss Cam's mouth. He pulled away, chuckling. "You smell of my butt."

"Sorry."

"Not complaining." Alex kissed him again before giving an enormous yawn.

"We should sleep. You have to get up early, right?"

"Yeah. Ugh. I need to set my alarm for seven." Alex heaved himself up off the bed, his reluctant limbs heavy with tiredness. He found his phone and set the alarm, leaving it on the floor by the bed. Then he put his boxers back on to sleep.

Cam put his underwear on too and they got back into bed together. After he'd turned off the lamp, Cam asked, "You want to cuddle?"

Warmth filled Alex. "Yeah."

"Big spoon or little spoon?"

"Little."

Alex rolled onto his side and Cam curved his body around him. With the weight of Cam's hand on his hip, and the warmth of his breath on the back of his neck, Alex had never felt more contented. The only intrusion was a tiny niggling voice at the back of his mind asking, *what happens now?* But Alex was tired enough to ignore it. He could worry about the consequences in the morning. Tonight he'd simply enjoy it.

FIFTEEN

Cam woke a little after nine with a nagging headache and a mouth that felt like a dirty carpet. It took him a moment to remember why he was on one side of the bed with a space beside him instead of sprawled in the middle as usual. When the events of the night before slotted into place in his sleep-addled brain, his stomach did a cartwheel.

His cock stiffened and he squeezed it through his boxers as disconnected memories of what they'd done together flashed into his mind. God, it had been good. Alex had been so sure of what he wanted, so receptive to everything they'd tried. Cam wished he'd been sober so he could recall every-thing more clearly, but he could remember enough to know that it was Alex who'd asked Cam to fuck him. And he knew without doubt that Alex had enjoyed it as much as he did.

Was it a mistake?

No. Cam couldn't regret what they'd done, but anxiety churned in his gut nevertheless. Where did they go from here, and what would it mean for their friendship? Cam had some thinking to do. He had to work out what the fuck he wanted so he could try and be honest with Alex at last.

Cam got up and pulled on some sweatpants and a T-shirt. Downstairs in the kitchen, he put the kettle on, and poured out a huge bowl of cereal and milk. Once he'd made tea he carried his mug and bowl through to the living room where Wicksy was still fast asleep on the sofa, snoring like a hippo.

"Jesus it stinks in here." Stale beer battled with the distinctive odour of farts. Cam put his stuff down on the coffee table and went to open a window.

"Ugh," Wicksy groaned, opening his eyes, and squinting at Cam. "I feel like shit."

"I'm not surprised. You were pretty pissed last night."

"I must have been if I crashed out here and stayed on the sofa all night." He sat up, pushing the heels of his hands into his eyes and rubbing. Then he looked blearily at Cam and frowned. "Where did Alex sleep? In my room?"

"No." Cam focused on his cereal, avoiding Wicksy's gaze. "In mine."

"Oh yeah?" Wicksy's tone was knowing. "About bloody time."

"What? We could have just slept together—as in really slept, not the euphemism."

"But you didn't though, did you?" Cam finally met Wicksy's eyes and his expression was gleeful. "I can tell because you're blushing."

"No I'm not," Cam replied pointlessly because his cheeks were indeed burning.

"Did you fuck?"

Cam glared at him. "None of your business."

"Dude. I'm happy for you. Seriously. Like I said, it's about bloody time you two pulled your heads out of your arses and dealt with the fact that you're meant to be together."

Raising his eyebrows, Cam said, "Since when were you such a romantic?"

"Since seeing you mooning over each other for months. You obviously like each other and fancy the pants off each other. It looks like the real deal to me, so why aren't you together yet? I mean, I get why you were wary at the beginning when you found out who his dad was, and with him only being seventeen. But things have changed since then."

"We're such good friends, though. I was worried about jeopardising that. Remember Leanne?"

"Yeah. But Alex isn't Leanne. And you're older and wiser and know what you want this time. Plus if you fucked last night, that ship has already sailed." Wicksy shrugged. "Things are complicated whatever happens. You can't take that back, so you might as well be honest with him, and take a fucking chance instead of being a pussy about it."

"Yeah. I suppose so."

It was tough love, but Cam had to admit he had a point. Last night had been incredible but it was also perhaps the catalyst he'd needed to force the issue about what the hell was going on with him and Alex. They needed to talk. It was high time that Cam admitted he had feelings for Alex and asked Alex what he wanted. Cam just had to hope that Alex wanted more than no-strings fun with him, because if he and Alex were going to be together Cam didn't want casual. He wanted commitment.

"So are you going to talk to him?"

"Yes. Later. He's at work till four."

RAINBOW PLACE STARTED off fairly quiet at the beginning of Alex's shift, as was usual on a Saturday morning, but gradually filled up as the town awoke. Alex was working as a server today and from around nine onwards, he was kept busy making endless cups of coffee and carrying food orders to the tables. His mood kept swinging wildly from high to low as complicated emotions swirled in his belly. Elation at what they'd done mingled with longing to do it again, along with a generous dash of anxiety about what was going to happen. Would Cam want to hook up again? Maybe now he'd take Alex up on the friends-with-benefits offer. Or would he back off and insist on going back to friends only? Alex sighed. He was past the point where he could only see Cam as a friend. Even if that was all that was on offer, Alex knew he'd never be satisfied with that. Not after last night.

They needed to talk, but there had been no time earlier —even if Cam had woken. As it was he'd been dead to the world despite Alex's alarm, and Alex had crept out without disturbing him. He wondered if Cam was awake yet, and if so—what he was thinking about the night before? He wanted to text Cam, but wasn't sure what he'd say. *Thanks for a great night* sounded trite, and the conversation they desperately needed to have wasn't one they could do by text. It would have to be face-to-face.

Distracted, Alex made a few mistakes with orders, which was unusual for him. After the third complaint, Seb took him aside.

"Is everything okay, Alex?"

"Yeah. Well, sort of. I don't know." There wasn't really time to explain the complexities of his love life when there were customers waiting to be served. "Things with Cam are a little complicated."

"Good complicated or bad complicated?"

"I'm not sure yet." Alex didn't dare let himself hope.

Seb studied him, his expression concerned. "Remember that if living there isn't helping the situation, my spare room is still yours if you want it. You can pick up an extra shift here each week in lieu of rent if that suits you?"

Alex ignored his knee-jerk reaction to refuse and considered what Seb was offering. "Yeah," he replied slowly. "Actually that might be a good idea. Thanks, Seb."

After last night, Alex knew he wouldn't be able to handle living there if Cam insisted on them just being friends again. With the undeniable attraction on both sides it would make things awkward. Although Alex had been the one to suggest they had some no-strings fun, in reality he had to admit that he couldn't do it. No matter how good the sex was, Alex needed more from Cam. Living there, the temptation would be too much, and Alex didn't want to end up in a situation where he was taking what he could get while constantly wanting more. Ultimately it would mess him up, and make him resent Cam, and Alex didn't want that.

And even if—Alex hardly dared hope—Cam decided he wanted more than friendship, it might still be better for them to have a little space while they redefined their relationship. Living on top of each other made things very intense, and if Alex wasn't under Cam's roof constantly it might take some of the pressure off and help things evolve more naturally between them.

"You're totally welcome." Seb smiled. "Right, I need to get back to work, and so do you. Please try and limit the cock-ups for the rest of the day."

"Yeah, I will. I'm sorry." Alex hung his head. He knew it

was bad for Seb's business if food or drinks got wasted because of his mistakes.

Seb patted Alex on the shoulder. "It happens to the best of us."

A LITTLE AFTER LUNCHTIME, Alex was delivering a tray full of coffees and cakes to a group of regulars—the silver allies as they liked to call themselves—a group of elderly ladies who had been staunch supporters of Rainbow Place ever since the day it had opened.

"Caramel latte?"

"That's yours isn't it, Marge?" One of the women said, sliding the cup across the table.

"And rainbow cake."

"Here please!" A woman with short, spiky, white hair that gave her the look of a dandelion seed head raised her hand. "Lovely. Thank you, dear." She beamed at Alex as he placed the plate in front of her.

"You're welcome. Enjoy."

As Alex turned to walk back to the kitchen, he froze at the sight of his mother. She was standing just inside the café door clutching her handbag and looking around nervously. Alex was trying to decide whether to greet her or make a dash to the kitchen before she saw him when the decision was taken away from him. Her eyes lit on him and she gave him a nervous smile.

Heart pounding, Alex tried to form his mouth into something approaching a smile, but he doubted it was remotely convincing. Rainbow Place was Alex's safe place. It had always been his refuge when he still lived at home, and now it was his workplace too. His mother's presence was jarring and made him bristle with resentment. *What the hell is she doing here?*

She started to approach, so Alex met her halfway.

"What do you want?" he asked abruptly. He knew he sounded rude, but he didn't think he owed her any respect. She'd sided with his father over him and had made no effort to contact him since he'd left home.

"I wanted to talk to you."

"You could have called. Maybe I don't want to talk to you."

"Alex, please." She put her hand on his arm.

He shook it off. "I'm busy working now anyway, so it's not a good time."

"Is everything okay, Alex?" Seb approached, looking warily at Alex's mum.

"Yeah. It's fine. I was just explaining to my mum that I'm too busy to talk to her."

She met his angry glare. He was surprised to see tears in her eyes, but her jaw was set with determination. "I can wait till the end of your shift if necessary." She moved to the nearest empty table, pulled out a chair, and sat.

Seb turned to Alex. "Do you want me to ask her to leave?"

"No. It's okay." Alex lowered his voice. "I'll talk to her in a bit if you don't mind me taking a break? But I want to let her stew for a while."

"Fine with me, on both counts." Seb grinned before going back to the till.

As Alex passed his mother's table she said, "Can I order a cup of tea?"

"You can. But you have to queue and pay at the bar. We don't take orders at the table."

"Oh, all right." She flushed. "I'll do that."

Alex made her wait for the tea as well as his company. About fifteen minutes after she'd ordered, he finally made his way to her table with a pot of tea for her and a latte for himself. Seb had said he could take as long as he needed, but Alex wanted to make this quick.

"Thank you," she said as Alex put teapot, cup and saucer, and milk in front of her.

He took the seat opposite with his coffee. "What have you got to say?" He leant back in his seat and folded his arms. Inside he was hurting but he refused to show her that.

"I wanted to say I'm sorry." She met his gaze without flinching and there was remorse in her expression. It wasn't enough. Alex waited for more. "I'm sorry for letting you down, for not supporting you when your father... when you fell out with him."

"You mean when he punched me in the face because he found out I was gay?"

She flushed. "Yes. That. He was wrong, Alex, and I was wrong not to stand up to him." She poured her tea with a trembling hand, and then added milk before continuing. "I've been reading things online, about sexuality, and about being an ally. I want to try to be better. I love you, Alex." Her eyes glittered with unshed tears. "You're my only son and I don't want to lose you."

"What about Dad? How does he feel?"

She shook her head, mouth tightening into a line. "I haven't talked to him about it. But I don't think his feelings have changed. He's angry. He doesn't understand and he doesn't want to try. But I do. If you'll let me?"

Alex felt his heart soften a little, thawing at the edges at least. "I suppose," he said cautiously. "What sort of thing are you thinking? I'm not coming to the house," he added. "Not as long as he's living there. Not unless he comes to me and apologises like you have, and even then I'm not sure I can be around him after what he did." He picked up his coffee and had a sip.

"I thought maybe we could meet sometimes, like this." She gave a small smile. "Just for coffee and a chat. I know it will take time for you to trust me again but we have to start somewhere."

As they stared at each other, Alex wary, his mother hopeful, Alex felt something shift. This level of honesty was new, and so was his mother treating him like an adult—like an equal who could make his own choices. Perhaps it would be possible to let go of the past and build a new relationship with her. "Does Dad know about this?"

Her face clouded. "No. But it has nothing to do with him. My relationship with you is *my* business," she said, eyes blazing.

Alex recognised a strength in his mother he'd never noticed before. He liked it. "Okay. Let's try."

"Oh, Alex, thank you," she gushed in relief. "Thank you for giving me a chance." Her smile was so bright and genuine that he couldn't help but respond by smiling back. There was an awkward pause, and then she asked, "So, tell me what's going on with you. Are you enjoying working here?"

While they finished their drinks, Alex told her about his job at Rainbow Place, and filled her in on how his studies were going. She listened and prompted him with the occasional question. When their cups were empty, Alex said, "I'd better get back to work in a minute."

"Where are you living now?" his mother asked. "You didn't mention that."

Alex hesitated. "I've been staying with some friends.

But I'm going to move in with Seb—the café owner—he has a spare room and he's offered it to me."

"Oh, okay. I'm glad you have somewhere. I don't blame you for not wanting to come home, but if you ever need money for rent then ask me. I'll help."

"Would Dad let you?" Alex raised his eyebrows. He couldn't imagine his father would condone that, and his mother didn't have her own income.

"I have some savings," she said. She lowered her voice, looking around as though afraid of being overheard. "There's some money I inherited from a great aunt that your father doesn't know about. I kept it separate."

"Why?"

"In case I ever want to leave him." There was that steely look of determination again.

"Are you planning on it?"

She gave a tiny shrug. "We'll see." Changing the subject, she said, "I'd better get going and let you get back to your job. Thank you for talking to me, and for saying we can meet again." She stood, picking up her handbag, and putting it over one shoulder.

"Text me." Alex stood too. "We can meet up again soon." He rather liked this new version of his mother who went against his father's wishes and who had secrets of her own. It would be interesting getting to know her better.

She approached him, and Alex tilted his cheek, expecting her usual air kiss. Instead she drew him into a hug, arms tight around him. He hugged her back, warmth unfurling in his chest at the unexpected affection. "I love you," she said quietly, so only he would hear.

Not ready to reply with *I love you too*, Alex squeezed her a little tighter. Maybe one day he'd be able to say it back.

CAM WAS a bundle of nerves by the time Alex was due back from work. Wicksy had made himself scarce to give them space to talk, heading out to play footy in the park with some of the rugby lads.

He'd given Cam a hug before leaving. "I'll probably go for a pint and have dinner at the pub after, so I won't be back till much later. Good luck, mate."

Unable to settle, Cam embarked on a pile of washing up in the kitchen. It was mostly Wicksy's, but at least it gave Cam something to do. After that he cleaned the sink, wiped all the counter tops, and had just started on the top of the cooker when he heard the sound of a key in the door. His heart surged, pounding hard as he heard Alex let himself in.

"Hi," Cam called.

"Oh, hey." Alex came into the kitchen and gave Cam a nervous smile. Looking around, he said, "Wow, you've been busy. I've never seen it looking so clean."

Cam tossed the cloth he was using into the sink and wiped his hands on a tea towel. "How was your day?"

"Okay, thanks. My mum came to see me."

"Oh shit. How did that go?" Cam had been shocked at the lack of contact from Alex's parents since he'd left home. Not his dad so much, and actually it was probably a good thing he'd left Alex alone. But his mum not even checking up on him to make sure he was okay seemed awful to Cam. Alex hadn't said much about it, but it had to hurt.

"It was okay I think. She was... different. She apologised for not supporting me, and admitted my dad was in the wrong. She's never done that before."

"Well that's good," Cam said cautiously. "Are you going to see her again?"

"Yeah. We're planning on meeting sometimes. I'm glad about that."

Silence fell between them and their gazes locked. Cam felt as though he was bursting with all the things that needed to be said but he didn't know where to start.

"We need—" he began at the same moment that Alex blurted, "Cam. I think we—"

They both stopped.

"You go first," Alex said.

Cam took a deep breath. "We need to talk."

Alex gave a nervous chuckle. "Yep. I'm glad we're on the same page about that, at least. Wanna go up to your room for privacy?"

"No need. Wicksy's out and won't be back for a while. Living room?"

"Okay."

Cam followed Alex into the living room where they sat at opposite ends of the sofa, angled to face each other. Alex's leg jiggled and he picked at his fingernails. He looked as stressed as Cam was.

"So." Cam wished he'd planned it out better. He knew how he felt, but hadn't worked out how to put it into words. "I know I've been saying I just want to be friends all this time.... But now I want more."

Alex raised his eyes to meet Cam's gaze, there was hope on his face, but it was wary too. "Why now? Because we fucked last night?"

"No," Cam said. "I've wanted more for a while but I was scared of what it would mean for our friendship. I kept trying to put distance between us and didn't want to admit my feelings were changing. Last night I got to the point where I couldn't fight it anymore. Then today I did a lot of thinking about what I wanted."

"And what do you want?" Alex's expression was intense; it felt as though he were looking right into Cam's soul.

"I want you, as a boyfriend. I want us to be in a relationship... *with* strings. When you suggested something casual it made me realise that wouldn't be enough for me. I can't do half measures with you, Alex. You came into my life as a friend, but the attraction was there from the start and it was hard to ignore. Then the more I got to know you, the more you mattered to me. I don't know exactly when I fell in love with you, but that's what this is. I love you, Alex, and I want to be with you—if you'll have me. I'm sorry it took me so long to get my head out of my arse and admit it."

Alex's lips curved into a small smile that widened, lighting up his face. "It did take you a while."

"So, what do you say?" Cam was on a knife edge, trying not to hope too much in case his dreams were dashed.

"Hmm. I might need some time to think about it." Alex's grin turned devilish.

Cam glared at him. "Alex!"

"Oh okay, okay. Yes. Of course it's a yes, idiot. Surely you know I've always wanted more than friendship. I did from the start and that never changed."

Relief and elation poured through Cam. "You had me worried there for a moment, you little shit."

"That's no way to talk to your boyfriend," Alex said. "Now get over here and kiss me."

Cam moved closer to Alex and cupped his jaw. All the joking and banter was gone now and they stared into each other's eyes with an intensity that gripped Cam's heart like a fist. "I meant what I said when I told you I loved you."

Alex pressed a gentle kiss to Cam's mouth. "I love you too."

Happiness swelled in Cam's chest. "Since when?"

"I don't know exactly. Does it matter?"

"No. I guess not." Cam kissed Alex and this kiss was anything but brief. As Alex's lips parted beneath his, their tongues touching, and breath mingling, nothing else in the world mattered other than the fact that Alex was in his arms, and was hopefully there to stay.

EPILOGUE

A month later

ALEX HAD a spring in his step as he and Cam walked down
the hill together into town. It was a Saturday morning and
Alex had the day off. He'd stayed at Cam's last night—as he
did about half the time. The rest of the time Cam slept over
with Alex at Seb's place. They often joked that they might as
well have stayed living together for the amount of time they
spent apart, but Alex moving in with Seb had been a good
decision overall. Alex had more room for his stuff, and a quiet
place to study when he needed it. And Cam and Wicksy had
a less-cluttered living room again. Maybe at some point in
the future Alex and Cam would want to get a place together,
but for now this arrangement worked perfectly.

He and Cam were going to meet his mother for lunch,
and although Alex was nervous about introducing them to
each other properly at last, he was excited too. Cam had
only met his mother the time they went to collect Alex's

stuff. Now Alex was on better terms with her, he was looking forward to introducing Cam as his boyfriend. She knew about Cam already, Alex had told her about him on one of their mother-son coffee dates, but having the three of them sitting down for a meal together would be pretty cool —Alex hoped.

"Maybe we should have arranged to meet somewhere other than Rainbow Place," Cam said as they walked. "Isn't it a bit weird going there to eat on your day off?"

"It doesn't bother me at all," Alex said. "Ever since it opened it's been my favourite place to hang out in Porthladock, and that hasn't changed because it's my workplace. I love it. I feel safe there." Not that he was expecting things to go badly with his mum meeting Cam, but something about being at Rainbow Place made Alex feel supported. In a space that was so clearly queer friendly, he could relax and be totally comfortable.

"Okay, cool. Well it's fine with me." Cam took his hand. "The food's always good, and your staff discount is a bonus."

Alex grinned sidelong at him. "Yeah. We might as well make use of it."

As weekends could be busy at lunchtime, Alex had asked Seb if he could save him a table. When they arrived, Seb pointed to a table in the corner set for three with a *Reserved* sign on it. Alex gave him a thumbs up and they took their seats and started to look at the menu.

"I don't know why I'm bothering to look because I already know I'm going to have the pork belly," Cam said. "It was amazing last time we ate here. I'm ruined for anything else."

"I'll probably go for the Cajun chicken burger." Alex

scanned the other options, even though he knew the menu by heart.

"Your mum's arrived," Cam said quietly.

Heart kicking up a notch, Alex raised his head to see his mother standing just inside the door looking around. He raised his hand and waved, returning her smile as she caught sight of him, and then stood to meet her as she crossed the room to where they were sitting. Cam stood too.

"Hello, darling," she greeted him warmly, hugging him tight as well as kissing him on the cheek. "And, Cam." She offered Cam her hand after releasing Alex. "It's good to see you again, under happier circumstances this time." Her cheeks pinked a little. Alex admired her for her honesty in not shying away from the past and the mistakes she'd made.

"Absolutely. Hello, Mrs Elliot."

"Sylvia, please." She patted his hand before letting go.

"Have a seat." Cam pulled out a chair for her.

"Thank you." She settled herself while they took the remaining seats. The table was a small one, pushed up against the wall on one side. Cam and Alex were opposite each other with Alex's mum between them.

She picked up the menu. "This all looks so lovely. I've only had cake here before. What would you recommend?"

"The pork belly is amazing," Cam said.

"It sounds it, but I think maybe something a little lighter...." She perused the menu. "I'll have the warm salmon salad. Do you boys know what you want? This is my treat."

"Are you sure?" Alex asked. "I get a discount, so you should let me order anyway."

"I say it's my treat—but I'm using the joint account to pay. And your dad can afford it without the discount."

"I'm sure he'd be thrilled to know he's paying for you to have lunch with me and my boyfriend," Alex said dryly.

"That's part of the satisfaction," she said. "And I'd better make the most of it because I won't have a joint account with him for much longer." She grinned at Alex, looking very pleased with herself as the words sank in.

"Mum... does that mean what I think it means?"

"I'm leaving him. I've seen a solicitor, I've found a place to rent near here, and I'm ready to go. I'm telling him tonight."

"Bloody hell!" Alex had hoped this might happen eventually, but he hadn't expected it so soon. "Do you need some moral support when you break it to him?"

"My solicitor will be there. Don't worry; I'm not taking any chances after what he did to you." Her face shadowed momentarily. "I knew he was controlling and difficult, but I never truly believed he could be violent. What happened with you changed everything once I stopped trying to make excuses for him. I can't live with him anymore."

Fierce pride swept through Alex. It couldn't have been an easy decision for her to make after years of letting him walk over her. "I'm glad you're doing this."

"Me too. I should have done it years ago. I'm sorry I didn't, Alex. That's my biggest regret."

"Better late than never." Although Alex couldn't help wondering how different his teenage years might have been if his mother had realised sooner what an arsehole his father was. But then if things had been different, maybe he'd never have met Cam.

"Anyway. What would you like to drink? I fancy champagne, this feels like a celebration."

"That sounds great," Cam said. "And you have good reason to celebrate."

"And it's one month exactly since we got together so there's another reason to celebrate too." Alex smiled at him. He didn't particularly like champagne, but he was all for letting his mum spend his dad's money on them while she still could.

"Right." His mum pushed her chair back and stood. "I'll go and order."

"Your mum is pretty awesome," Cam said as they watched her walk over to the bar.

"Yeah." A strength and spirit she'd kept hidden for a long time was emerging, constantly surprising Alex. The news that she was leaving his dad was wonderful.

His mother returned from the bar once she'd ordered, and soon afterwards Seb came over with a bottle of champagne and three glasses on a tray. He popped the cork and poured out a little for Alex's mum to taste.

"Perfect," she said.

When all their glasses were full, she raised hers. "Here's to new beginnings." She clinked her glass with both of theirs.

Alex met Cam's gaze. "To new beginnings," they echoed, each taking a sip before smiling at each other.

AFTER A LEISURELY LUNCH followed by coffee, they walked Alex's mum to her car where it was parked in the town centre car park. Alex's mum hugged him, and then opened her arms to Cam too.

"Thank you," she said, drawing back so she could look him in the eye. "Thank you for looking after my boy when I let him down."

"You're welcome," Cam said gruffly.

"And thank you for making him happy." She glanced at Alex and he saw her eyes were bright with tears.

A rush of emotion stole Alex's breath for a moment, making his eyes prickle too. He gave her a wobbly smile. "Good luck with Dad tonight. If you need us, just call."

"I'll be fine, but thank you for the offer. Let's meet again soon and I can tell you how it went. Maybe lunch next week? Or dinner even, once I'm settled into my flat."

"That would be great."

"Right." Her smile was strong again. "Take care of yourselves, and I'll see you soon. Bye." She opened her car door and climbed in.

"Bye, Mum." Alex closed it for her.

They stood shoulder to shoulder and watched as she drove away.

"Wow." Alex shook his head. "I can't believe how much has changed in such a short time."

Cam took his hand. "Want to walk along the front before we head home? I could use the exercise after all that delicious food."

"Sure."

Walking hand in hand with Cam through Porthladock was still a novelty, and gave Alex a thrill of pride and nerves combined every time. Most people didn't bat an eyelid, but they got the occasional curious or disapproving glance. Those small negatives were balanced out by people who smiled at them after noticing their joined hands.

"Can we sit for a minute?" Alex asked when they reached the bench where they'd sat that first night, after the opening of Rainbow Place.

Cam let Alex draw him down and they sat close together, looking out at the view. Alex loved how it changed with the seasons. Today the water was a dark-greyish blue, reflecting the cloudy sky above. White horses of foam danced on the waves, whipped up by a stiff autumn breeze. A few intrepid dinghy sailors zoomed across the estuary, boats leaning at a perilous angle.

Chilled by the wind, Alex shuffled nearer to Cam, who put his arm around him.

Taking a quick look around, and seeing that although there were other people around, nobody was watching them, Alex pressed a quick kiss to Cam's cheek.

Cam turned and smiled. "You okay?"

"I'm very, very okay." Alex grinned back. Heart full to the brim with happiness and hope, he kissed Cam full on the lips, and Cam kissed him back. It felt right that they'd come full circle to this bench. Five months after they'd shared their first kiss they were back, and this time around Alex didn't have to be unsure of Cam's feelings.

He knew there were many more kisses as sweet as this one in their future.

ABOUT THE AUTHOR

Jay lives just outside Bristol in the West of England. He comes from a family of writers, but always used to believe that the gene for fiction writing had passed him by. He spent years only ever writing emails, articles, or website content.

One day, Jay decided to try and write a short story—just to see if he could—and found it rather addictive. He hasn't stopped writing since.

Jay is transgender and was formerly known as she/her.

www.jaynorthcote.com
Twitter: @Jay_Northcote
Facebook: Jay Northcote Fiction

MORE FROM JAY NORTHCOTE

Nothing Special
Nothing Ventured
Not Just Friends
Passing Through
The Little Things
The Dating Game – Owen & Nathan #1
The Marrying Kind – Owen & Nathan #2
The Law of Attraction
Imperfect Harmony
Into You
Cold Feet
What Happens at Christmas
A Family for Christmas
Summer Heat
Tops Down Bottoms Up
The Half Wolf
Secret Santa
Second Chance

Made in the USA
Middletown, DE
18 November 2019